25

Ben and Blackbeard

By the same author

The Mercury Cup

T. R. BURCH

Ben and Blackbeard

Illustrated by Susan Neale

A DRAGON BOOK

GRANADA
London Toronto Sydney New York

Published by Granada Publishing Limited in 1983

ISBN 0 583 30569 5

A Dragon Original
Copyright © T. R. Burch

Granada Publishing Limited
Frogmore, St Albans, Herts AL2 2NF
and
36 Golden Square, London W1R 4AH
515 Madison Avenue, New York, NY 10022, USA
117 York Street, Sydney, NSW 2000, Australia
100 Skyway Avenue, Rexdale, Ontario, M9W 3A6, Canada
61 Beach Road, Auckland, New Zealand

Printed and bound in Great Britain by
Hazell Watson & Viney Ltd, Aylesbury, Bucks
Set in Plantin

Granada ®
Granada Publishing ®

Chapter One

Ben had just enough time to take in a supply of air before he hit the water. He went down, jack-knifed, rose gasping to the surface. He could see no sign of Isobel and Jane.

It was all his own fault. He knew that. He had built his raft out of an old door, some worm-eaten planks, and a couple of rusty oil-drums. It had been good enough for some trial trips on the stream. At least, it had all stayed together. He'd been pleased with it, and with himself for building it.

Then he had asked his sisters if they would like a ride – and that had been his great mistake. Things were bound to go wrong when Isobel and Jane were involved.

Jane had come because she didn't want to be left out, but she had brought a book with her to show that she was not particularly excited by what she called Ben's silly passion for the stream.

Everything had been all right to begin with. The stream was shallow, only a foot or two deep, confined within high banks so that the trees hung over and made a dark green tunnel, mysterious, almost ghostly. He had had to work hard to get any speed out of it at all. He nearly lost the pole once, when it stuck in the soft mud at the side, but he managed to pull it out before Isobel noticed any-

thing wrong. Jane, of course, never noticed anything.

And then the water rose, gradually at first, then in a sudden surge which took Ben by surprise.

Where had it all come from? There it was, rushing down as though someone had opened a gate, and the raft rose with it so that the pole was only just long enough to reach the bottom.

At any rate, he didn't have to work so hard to keep the raft moving: the current was doing all that for him. So long as he kept it in the middle of the stream, right away from the high slippery banks, they were all right. Once, they had hit the side where a tree's roots stuck out black and slimy, and the raft had gone round and round as though caught in a whirlpool, but he got it straight again.

He had never seen the stream as full as this before. It had rained a lot yesterday, so much that he hadn't even wanted to go out. He knew that the stream drained the fields all round: perhaps a drain somewhere had got blocked, and the water had built up until the pressure was too great for the mud and old leaves, and it had all come pouring out, all at one go. The sluice gates, Ben knew, because he had often climbed along them, were as rotten as old biscuits.

Ben put out a hand to sweep away the trailing branches of a weeping willow. The water was only a foot from the top of the bank just here. It looked thick and muddy and evil. The raft whirled away from the willow and out into the middle of the stream.

'You're going too fast,' Jane told him.

Ben merely grunted.

''Ware rocks on the starboard bow!' Isobel called out suddenly.

Ben looked up. 'That's timber,' he said. 'And it's on the portside.' He waggled the pole in his hands to steer the raft round the obstruction.

Isobel grabbed one of the planks as they sped past.

'It's full of rusty nails,' she said.

'You'll scratch yourself, get poisoned, and die in horrible agonies,' Ben told her, but without much hope. No such luck.

Ben went on with his steering with dogged obstinacy. He knew there was a tricky bit coming up, a bend in the stream, almost a right angle, sharp and unexpected. There was usually a bit of a muddy shore just at this point, sloping gently to the corner, but with the water as high as it was now, the shore would be covered. The danger was that the raft would ground in the submerged mud. Ben tried to remember just how far the shelving bank reached.

More willow trees. With irritation Ben pushed the long whippy trailing branches out of the way. That idiot Isobel was trying to catch them, and this upset the smooth progress of the raft. He shouted at her, but she just looked like a mule and went on doing it.

He could see the bend now. As he expected, the water was almost up to the lip of the bank, and the shelf of mud in the corner was invisible. The rush of the water was hitting the corner with a sound like distant thunder. He would have to steer well clear of it, make a quick turn to the left as soon as he could, or they'd end up stuck like snails in the slime.

'Ready to fend off!' he called out to Isobel.

'Where?'

'The corner. Keep the bows away from the bank on the right. It'll be a near thing.'

'I can't reach that far,' Isobel objected.

'Use that plank. Only mind the nails.'

Ben watched as she crouched ready to push the plank into the mud. They were nearly at the bend already. A few seconds to go. The roar of the racing water filled his ears.

'Now!' he shouted. He swung the pole, felt the drag of the stream, pushed against it, held on.

'Made it!' he yelled triumphantly. The raft was round the corner and nothing had scraped bottom. 'It's plain sailing now. Nice long straight stretch.' He sat back on his heels. He could afford to relax again, even if the speed of the water was greater than anything he remembered from the past. He was enjoying himself.

Then he suddenly thought of the bridge. 'You'll have to duck down when we get to it.'

'Get to what?'

'The bridge. It's wooden, just half a dozen planks, with a couple of supports at an angle to the bank. You'll soon see.'

Jane peered ahead, as though she was looking for some far distant shore after a long sail across an unknown sea. 'Not yet.'

Ben narrowed his eyes. 'Funny. Can't be far.

There's a bit of a bend just ahead, but you can usually see it from here. There! Look out!'

Desperately he began to slow the raft by pushing the pole against the steep clay sides. He was afraid he might lose it, and he didn't dare push too hard. Perhaps he could grab at some tree roots and hang on, so long as he didn't part company with the raft.

'What's the matter?' Isobel called out, alarmed by his sudden energy.

'The bridge. It's down! I never did think those supports were much good. The whole thing's collapsed.'

Ben gazed ahead to the black mass of timber which had been the bridge. He hadn't much time. In another few seconds they'd be crashing into it. The tangled planks had piled up the water behind them, and it was roaring over the top like a burst dam. The raft would hit it like a bullet unless he could do something to slow it down. A picture sprang into his mind. The raft would capsize, would throw them over the remains of the bridge. Jane would lose her book. Suppose one of them got caught beneath those slabs of timber? Suppose the water rushed over them as they struggled to free themselves, kicking against the current and the drowned bridge until they stopped because they were too tired to go on fighting?

Ben forced the picture from his mind. He had to concentrate on the raft. There was an overhanging tree a few yards ahead. He could jump for it, crawl along that branch to safety . . . except that Jane and

Isobel would never make it. No, he had to try to stop the raft before it broke against the bridge.

Again he pushed the pole into the soft clay of the bank, fighting against the force of the water until his muscles ached. The raft spun half round and the pole broke free. He had a brief sight of Isobel's face, white and frightened. And Jane. She was clutching the book to her chest, her eyes wide, staring.

The raft rushed on. To Ben's scared mind it seemed to increase its speed as it neared the bridge. He could already see the individual planks, black and mud-stained, with white lines where the timber had cracked. They stuck up like jagged teeth, rotten with age and neglect.

'Look out!' he yelled, but he didn't think they were listening. Their eyes, like his, were fixed on the black lumps in the rushing water. Well, he thought, at least Jane couldn't say she'd been bored.

The bridge came roaring to meet them. A clang of metal – that was an oil-drum. Then they were spinning, tilting, falling. One of the oil-drums was over the edge, but one at the back was still caught. The raft stuck crazily in mid-air with the thunder of the water all round it. Then with a crack like a gun, it was free. Free and falling. And they were falling with it.

And then they were in the water, gasping for air. Ben struggled with the seething water. Where were Isobel and Jane?

But all he could see as he thrashed and fought with the stream was a face.

A bearded face, a picture in black and white. Narrow eyes staring at him coldly.

Then the water covered him again.

Chapter Two

Isobel was furious. She stood on the bank, shaking with cold and temper, and screamed at Ben.

'It was all your fault!' she kept on shouting. 'All your fault!' Jane had already retreated.

Ben said nothing. He knew that when Isobel got into one of her tempers, there was nothing he could do about it except keep out of the way and hope she soon calmed down. He was wondering whether he would ever be able to save his raft, and he had no time to spare for Isobel. He had spent days making that raft; he'd been proud of it; he'd given it a series of trials on the stream, before the water rose the way it had done in the last hour, and it had behaved perfectly. Isobel had nagged him for a ride, and he had agreed to take her. Jane had come because even if she wasn't interested she didn't like being left out.

The raft.

It was upside down, but at least it was still afloat. One corner was wedged against a tree root and a fallen plank from the bridge, and the water roared past it without any effect. Ben was glad of that. If he could reach the other side, he might be able to rescue it. That overhanging tree was in just the right place to give him something to hold on to.

He looked at the remains of the bridge. Now that it had collapsed, it made a solid dam of twisted

timber. It looked safe enough to clamber over. He could see the planks below the level of the stream which rushed and poured over the lip like a miniature waterfall. After the last five minutes he could hardly get any wetter than he was. He wasn't worried about wet clothes; his jeans and check shirt would dry of their own accord if he forgot about them.

He glanced at Isobel. Her shrieks were less loud than they had been, but she was still grumbling as she tried ineffectually to wring the water out of her jeans. Jane was sitting in the sunshine with her back to a tree, her wet clothes spread out neatly on the grass in front of her. She was quite happy: she had thrown the book she had been reading onto the bank just before the raft hit the bridge, and now she was again involved in it. She looked up once at the raging Isobel.

'Shut up, Bel,' she said, with a younger sister's privilege. 'Can't you see Ben wants some help with his raft?' She made no attempt herself to get up and offer help.

Isobel glared, almost speechless. 'But I'm wet!' she insisted.

'Probably something to do with the water. Don't make a fuss, Bel. Run about a bit, and you'll soon be dry. Why don't you run to the end of the field and back? There's a cow over there, but it won't hurt you. At least, I think it's a cow.'

Isobel sat down on the grass and at once shot up again.

'And that,' Jane said kindly, 'is a thistle. Honestly, Isobel, you'd be much better off helping Ben.'

'Bel!' Ben called out. 'I'm going to try getting over the other side. The trouble is that if I loosen the raft, it'll just go floating off on its own and we'll lose it. So I'll tie some rope to it – I can take a piece off one of the oil-drums – throw it over to you, so that when the raft's free, you can haul it over here. Right?'

Isobel could think of nothing rude enough to say, so she stayed silent and watched as Ben put one foot cautiously onto the tumbled bridge.

'It feels firm,' he said.

'You'll fall in.'

'Shut up.'

Ben started to crawl along the wreckage. The planks which stuck above the stream made good hand-holds, and he felt completely secure. Half-way across he suddenly thought of the black-bearded face he had glanced just before he hit the water. Well, if there *was* someone about, he might have the decency to come and help. But there was no sign of the man now.

He crawled on until he had almost reached the other bank and then jumped. He felt the timbers move under him as he leapt, but the whole tangled structure was still there when he looked back to see. Gradually he worked his way down the bank, holding on to a branch of the overhanging tree until one foot reached the raft. It wobbled beneath his weight as he eased himself onto it, but did not escape the root which held it fast. He knelt in the centre of the raft and began to work at the knots which kept the rope in place. A pity he'd made them so tight, but it was too late to worry about that now. One fingernail broke, and he sucked his finger for a moment or two before attacking the rope with renewed energy. He wished he had a knife, though it was probably better he'd left his pocket-knife at home today or he'd have lost it when he was thrashing about in the water. It would have gone rusty, too.

The rope began to yield to his picking and pushing, then the knot slipped, and he sat back with a coil of it in his hands. The freed oil-drum gently slipped downstream and was caught by the main current. Ben wasn't worried about that: he knew where to get another one. It was the door which formed the main body of the raft, and that was what he wanted to save. Unwanted doors were scarce.

He tied one end of the rope to a plank, then threw the other end towards Isobel on the far bank. The first time he tried, it fell short, but he coiled it up like a cowboy's lariat and tried again. Isobel caught it with surprising ease. Ben grunted with satisfaction.

'Hang on!' he shouted, as Isobel began to pull. 'Wait till I've freed it.'

As he clung to the tree, he kicked out with one foot. Suddenly the raft was free, and his feet slid away from him. He yelled, but Isobel was too busy pulling to notice a mere brother. Ben's legs splashed in the water like a netted fish. Just his luck, he thought. A second ducking. He scrambled through the mud and sticky clay to the safety of the bank.

At least the raft was safe. He watched as Isobel drew it across the stream and landed it.

'Tie it to that bush,' Ben called out.

'What did you think I was going to do? Are you coming back this side?'

'I shall have to. Got to see you two home.'

Jane looked up briefly and gave him a glare of contempt. Ben cautiously tried his weight on the collapsed bridge. He'd crawled over before, but this time he thought he'd take it at a run. Four steps, then a jump – that ought to do it. He made three of the steps, then slipped, stumbled, almost fell, gathered all his strength together for the final jump.

He landed on the edge with his face in the wet earth and his ankles in the stream. He rolled over and looked at the sky.

Well, he'd made it. He decided to ignore Isobel's cackles of laughter.

Jane suddenly shut her book and said she was hungry.

'This,' Ben said dreamily, 'is a desert island. You'll have to make a line and catch fish. Otherwise you'll starve.'

'I'm going home,' said Jane, dragging on her jeans.

'No chance. Not a sign of a sail. All that'll be left in a few days will be a pile of whitening bones, picked clean by the seagulls.'

'Goodbye,' Jane said. 'If you want to lie there catching your death of cold, that's your affair. Me, I'm going to get some dry clothes.'

'She's right,' Isobel agreed.

'I thought we were going to sail down to the town and buy some food there,' Ben said. He sat up and began to watch the stream. 'We did it just in time, you know. That dam isn't going to last much longer.' He put out a hand and tugged at one of the planks. It came loose, and he heaved it into the water and watched it go careering away.

'You do that,' Isobel said, 'and there's going to be one enormous wave as all that water gets free.'

Ben considered. It was worth trying. Experimentally he tugged at another plank. The whole structure shuddered and shook. Another plank, and it ought to go, Ben thought. He was right.

The stream roared and foamed around the wreckage of the bridge. A great wall of water surged between the high banks, hitting the raft with a thud which brought Ben to his senses. He leapt for the rope which Isobel had tied to the bush, hoping that the knot she had used was not one of her usual grannies. He was surprised to find that the knot held. The raft kicked and bucketed and dragged, but the rope was strong enough to keep it to the bank.

Gradually the level subsided, and the raft was left at an angle, one end of it one metre higher than the other.

'I'm going,' Jane said again and marched off, clasping the book to her chest. Ben looked at the raft regretfully. He'd have to go home anyway to get another oil-drum, so there was nothing else he could do here.

Isobel was already following Jane, and Ben fell in behind, pushing his hands into the pockets of his soaked jeans. A thought suddenly struck him.

'Bel!' he called out. 'We're all wet.'

'He's a genius, that boy,' Isobel said to the air.

'No, but Bel, there's going to be a row.'

'Why?'

'Well, wet clothes, and all that.'

'Jane and I will go home and change.'

'I know Mum's out all day, but they won't be dry by this evening. Not really dry, and she won't like it if she finds out you fell in.'

'That's why we're not going to tell her. They got a

bit dirty, that's all, so we decided to wash them to save her the extra work.'

'Do you think she'll believe it?'

'Course.'

'Then you can do mine as well. All right, Bel?'

'No,' Isobel said firmly. 'You do your own cleaning up.'

Ben trudged on in silence. That was sisters for you. It was all very well Mum saying he had to be the man of the family now and look after his sisters, but what was the point when you had sisters like that? He should have let them drown.

It was only ten minutes' walk to the house. Isobel had already fetched the backdoor key from under the brick at the side of the shed where it was always kept, and she was in the kitchen putting the kettle on to boil when Ben arrived.

'Don't drop water all over the floor,' she said. 'I'm making a hot drink. Do you want some?'

'OK.'

'Then go and find some dry clothes.'

Ben glowered. Just because she was a year older than he was didn't give her the right to behave like an aunt. Still, she was probably right.

His room was in the attic. It was an old house, with small windows sticking out of a steep roof. As Ben found some dry clothes he looked through the window. He could see the river gleaming in the distance like a silver snake in the sunlight. Funny there had been that much water in it today. A combination, he supposed, of yesterday's rain and the dam formed by the collapsed bridge. Perhaps

the gates of the mill-pond a mile upstream had gone as well. He'd have to go and see this afternoon. He'd take his camera with him and see if he could get a shot of it. His camera was one of the instant sort which produced a picture almost at once, and Ben, who had got it for his birthday a month before, was very proud of it.

He felt more comfortable now that he was dry. Perhaps if he took his wet clothes down with him, Isobel would relent and wash them for him. It would be worth trying.

He found her at the kitchen sink, pummelling soggy material with a wooden stick. 'Bring them over here,' she said, without turning round.

Ben grinned. Sisters weren't so bad, after all. He sat opposite Jane who had a book in one hand and a steaming mug in the other. He took one of the other two mugs and enjoyed the smell of it.

'That's good,' he said. Flattery, he thought, didn't cost anything.

'You've got five minutes to drink it,' Isobel said.

'Why?'

'Because Jane's lost her necklace.'

'The St Christopher one?'

'Yes, and she wants it back.'

'Well, where did she lose it?'

'The stream.'

Ben laughed. 'If you think I'm going to go diving into that lot after Jane's necklace, you're wrong.'

'It's not *in* the stream. She says she knows she had it after she got out of the water, because she remembers playing with it while she was sitting under that tree. The clasp must have been loose, and it fell off there.'

'Well, if she knows where it is, she can go and get it,' Ben said.

'Do you want your jeans washed or not?'

'Oh, all right.'

'Five minutes, then.'

Sisters, Ben thought resentfully. They shouldn't be allowed. He took his time over the coffee, just to show his independence, then ambled off, swinging the strap of his camera over his shoulder. It wouldn't take long to get back to the bridge. He'd search for a few minutes, and if he couldn't find the necklace, well, it wasn't his fault . . . Jane ought to be more careful.

Ben found it almost at once. It lay on the short grass beneath the tree and winked at him. He picked it up, stuffed it in his pocket, and began to walk upstream.

It was then that he realised there was something odd about the tree on the other bank, the tree to which he had clung when he had freed the raft.

A man stood in its shadow, black against the trunk. There was no movement. Just a round white face and a black beard.

Chapter Three

Ben stood absolutely still. He knew it was the same man. He could remember the exact second when he had seen that face before, peering down at him as the raft tipped over the edge of the broken bridge and threw him into the stream. He had thought to himself at the time: all right, we can all swim. We'll get wet, but there's no real danger, not unless the bridge chooses this moment to break up. And, whatever happens, there's a man up there on the bank who will be prepared to lend a hand.

But it had not happened like that. Isobel and Jane and he had pulled themselves out of the water without any help. When he had looked again, the man was no longer there.

Ben's gaze travelled over the stream. The level was lower now that the dam had gone, more like its normal self. The raft was still there, tilted at a crazy angle against the bank. It would make a good picture like that, if he got the light and the distance right. For a couple of minutes he concentrated on the camera. The result, when he looked at it, was disappointing: a couple of pieces of wood floating in a stream, and a door hanging by a rope from a bush. So what?

He stuffed the square picture in the back pocket of his jeans and wandered away. He was going to the mill. There might be a better picture there, if the gates really had broken.

Suddenly he remembered the bearded face across the stream. He turned to look, and his eyes searched the whole bank, but there was no sign of him under the tree or anywhere else.

Odd, that. He must have recognised him, known that the boy fiddling with the camera was the same one who had fallen in the stream an hour before. You'd have expected him to say something, even if it was only 'hello'.

Still, he was no longer there, so it didn't matter.

Ben strode along the bank. He had to push his way through bushes and knee-high grass most of the way. There was a path, but it ran along the other side of the stream, and he didn't feel like wading across and ruining another set of clothes. Isobel's good nature was not going to last long – nor, come to think of it, would their mother be all that pleased. She was out most days, working at her job in the town, so the three of them had plenty of freedom when the school holidays came round. There were limits, though, to how far you could go.

The grass flapped wet against his ankles as he walked on. He had rolled the bottoms of his jeans up to his knees to save them, and they felt uncomfortable round his legs, but he had to put up with it. He'd soon be there. Just round the next bend.

The mill was one of his favourite places. Nobody had lived there for years now, and the great wheel would never turn again. It was a two-storeyed building, weather-boarded, black with tar and age.

Little windows looked sightlessly out on the surrounding ring of trees. There was no glass left in them, and birds flew in and out without fear of interruption. The inside was dark, gloomy, dusty, with rotten floorboards which groaned and shivered under your feet and made you think somebody must be there. All the machinery had been taken away, leaving an empty barn of a place where bats huddled in the rafters.

Outside the building was a pond with a wooden gate behind which the stream built up until it had gained enough pressure to turn the wheel. Ben had been watching it gradually rotting away ever since he could remember, and now he saw that his guess had been right. The heavy rains of yesterday had finally broken through the spongy boards of the gate, and the stream had run free and high, as they had seen it earlier that morning. Now the level was down, and all that remained of the pond was a broad expanse of sticky black mud which smelled of decaying weeds. An old pram stuck up in the middle, upside down.

Ben was interested in that pram. It must, he thought, have been there for years, but the wheels still looked good. He might be able to use them on a go-cart, or a truck, or something of that sort. Pairs of wheels always came in handy.

He stood on the edge of the mud and estimated the distance. Seven metres at least. And plenty of dirt to wade through. Fortunately, the stream, now reduced to a few yards in width, was beyond the pram, so he didn't have to find a way to cross that.

But there was still the mud. He took off his sandals and rolled his jeans even further up his legs. Mud on his skin didn't matter, mud on his jeans did after this morning's little adventure.

Mud oozed between his toes like black toothpaste from a tube. It felt cold and slimy. Little bubbles of air grew on its surface and burst with a faint plop. He wondered whether there were any eels buried in the slime, and if so, how he could catch one. His thoughts were distracted by the fact that one leg was deep in the mud, almost up to his knee. He pulled it out, amused by the sucking and bubbling noises which the mud produced when he disturbed it, and he waded back to dry land. Thoughtfully he tugged out a handful of long grass and rubbed some of the dirt off his legs.

He needed some sort of bridge. His eyes searched the bank for old planks or perhaps a fallen dead branch which he could throw across the slime.

Nothing.

Planks. There were plenty of old planks lying about inside the mill. It shouldn't need too much force to rip a few of them away from their rusty nails and drag them out here.

Ben pushed his grimy feet into his sandals and went round the building to where the door had once been. It was just a black and gaping hole now. Experimentally he pulled at some of the boards with

which the building was covered, but they were thick and tough and immovable. He slipped into the gloom inside, waiting for a moment until his eyes became accustomed to the dark after the bright sunshine outside.

As he had thought, there were plenty of planks to choose from. A great ragged hole stretched across the centre where the old machinery had been ripped away, and it was an easy job to prise up one or two of the floorboards. Nobody was going to miss them.

He staggered out, dragging the plank behind him. It clattered over the doorstep and the rough track which led to the pond. In a few minutes he had three of them at the edge of the mud. He pushed one out over the oozing surface and tried his weight on it. Firm as a rock. Well, almost.

That pram certainly looked a fine sight, sticking up there in a sea of sludge. The mud on its frame was already dry, grey rather than black, and beginning to crack. It'd make a good picture. He raised the camera to his face and took the shot. It wasn't as funny when the square snap came out of the box. He was disappointed at the waste of film, and pushed the picture into his pocket with no more than a glance.

The camera. He'd better not go crawling over his home-made bridge with that slung round his neck, just in case he did fall in. He could leave it near the wall of the mill. Safe enough there. His sandals could go there as well.

With another hitch to his jeans he prepared to extend his floating bridge by pushing the second plank over the first until it plopped into the ooze beyond. He grunted with satisfaction, and began to whistle to himself. Another plank, and he'd be there.

The third plank sank a little beneath his weight, but no more than he expected, and certainly not enough to cause him any alarm. He reached the pram without difficulty and began to drag it towards the bank. It didn't want to come, but he worked at it with his hands, cleaning away the weed and drying mud, until it began to move. After that it was easy, crawling backwards along his bridge, pulling the pram upside down with him. No problem.

Ben sat on the bank and cleaned his hands in the grass. He had plenty of time. He could poke away all that mud on the pram with a stick. He was still whistling as he worked. The two axles which held the pairs of wheels were beginning to appear through their covering of sludge.

It must have been a loud bang which startled him. He had been so absorbed in his work that no rustle of leaves or twitter of birds would have been enough to make him lose his concentration.

Something had banged.

A plank falling? Or wood breaking? A door slamming?

There were no doors at the mill, only empty holes where the wind could play undisturbed.

Ben sat back on his heels, completely still. He was waiting for another bang so that he could make certain that he really had heard it and could discover from which direction it came.

Nothing.

Still, he knew it wasn't a door, and he was curious by nature. Cautiously he rose and padded quietly back to the mill. His bare feet fell silently on the soft damp grass. His eyes and ears were alert for any movement, any sound. He could hear the patter of leaves in the trees, could see the quiet motion of the branches in a light breeze.

He put out a hand to the gnarled boarding of the mill when he reached it and stopped. Was that the sound of footsteps on the other side of the building? Who was it sneaking about in the undergrowth like a thief?

It occurred to him that it might be Isobel, come to see if he had done his job and found Jane's necklace. So she didn't trust him, was that it? Right.

He crept along the side of the mill, expecting to find Isobel just round the corner. She was going to discover what it meant to come spying on him.

He advanced one eye round the sharp angle of the building and saw nothing but green grass and dark brown trunks. Again he trod softly along the line of the mill to the next corner. He remembered that there was an overgrown area of gravel at the back. If anyone walked on that, he'd be bound to hear. His feet met the sharpness of stone and he paused at the corner while his eyes travelled slowly round the circle of the clearing. Tree trunks like well-spaced columns with green umbrellas at the top; a darker hole where a narrow track led away from the mill through the trees; and a tall figure standing there, as still as stone.

31

Ben crouched against the base of the wall. He had not been heard, he was sure of that, for the tall figure made no movement. He had time to note the shape of the head, the breadth of the shoulders. The man was wearing brown corduroy trousers and a brown coat. Ben could not see his face, but he was sure that the man had a beard.

Then the man turned, slowly, quietly, and looked straight at him. Ben's muscles stiffened but he made no attempt to dart back. If he did, he knew, the sudden action would attract the man's attention at once. He hoped his faded jeans and dark-coloured shirt would not show up against the boards of the mill, but it was a small hope. Anyway, what had he got to be afraid of? It was just that never before had he seen anyone at the mill. It had been his private place of retreat, and he was not keen on intruders.

The man's eyes seemed to pass over him and beyond. Ben breathed again, and blinked. When he looked again the man had gone.

Ben was startled. The man must have just melted into the trees, he thought, and he didn't like it. He had felt safer when he could see where the fellow was. He straightened, walked out into the clearing, keeping to the clumps of grass because of his bare feet.

No, nobody there. Perhaps he had just imagined it.

He crept round to the far side of the mill. He'd been all the way round now, and there wasn't a soul to be seen. He poked his head through one of the empty windows and peered into the darkness.

Something caught his eye in the gloom, and he quietly hoisted himself up and over the window sill and dropped to the floor.

A shaft of sunlight fell like a solid column into the middle of the great room, making a white diamond shape on the boards. One of the planks showed pale where he had broken it off, but that was all.

Ben wandered out into the sunshine and back to the pram. As soon as he got there, he knew there was something wrong. Not with the pram, or the muddy pond, or the three planks he had stretched across the slime. No, it was something further back, something he had seen but taken no notice of at the time.

He spun round to face the mill.

His sandals were there, just where he had left them at the base of the wall. But the camera had gone.

Chapter Four

He didn't tell Isobel at once. He had given Jane the St Christopher necklace, and she was only mildly grateful. She and Isobel were busy cooking baked beans on toast when he arrived home, and he was able to slip past them without them noticing the state of his feet. The pram wheels were safely lodged in the shed outside where Ben kept things he didn't want interfered with.

When he came downstairs again, cleaner and tidier, he slid into his place at the kitchen table and reached for the tomato sauce.

'What's after?' he asked.

He was told to wait and see. Isobel tended to become secretive when she thought she was in charge. She looked at him with sudden suspicion.

'What have you been doing?'

'Nothing much. Walking.'

'What else?'

'Took a bit of time finding Jane's necklace.'

'And then?'

'Nothing. I told you.'

'You didn't come straight in.'

Ben sighed. This was like being back at school. What were holidays for? Something about freedom, and doing what you wanted, wasn't it? And not being badgered by a sister who was only a year older, anyway.

'I found some wheels. Off an old pram.'

'Where?'

'Up by the mill.'

Isobel seemed satisfied. Jane looked up from her plate. Isobel didn't allow her to read while she was eating, so for once she knew what they were talking about.

'Is the raft still all right?'

'It's safe. I'll rescue it this afternoon. I took a picture of it.'

'Let's see.'

Ben pulled the square photograph out of his back pocket, and Jane studied it critically. 'You'll have to do something about mending it before you get me on that thing again,' she remarked.

Ben had no intention of letting either of them anywhere near his raft, but he thought it better not to say so.

'What's that other photo you've got?'

Reluctantly Ben passed it over. 'Just the pram.'

'What's it in? All that dark stuff.'

'Mud,' Ben said briefly, but Jane wasn't satisfied with that, and he had to tell her about the mill-pond and the home-made bridge.

Isobel put out a hand for the photograph. 'You fell in again,' she said accusingly.

'No, I didn't. I've got too much sense.'

Isobel laughed. 'I thought there was a funny smell when you walked in. Well, I'm not washing any more of your jeans, so there.'

'I didn't ask you to, and there's no need.'

Isobel looked disappointed. 'It's not very clear,' she said critically, looking at the photograph.

'A bit too far away.'

'What's this sort of white blob at the back? Looks like somebody's face.'

'What? Where? There isn't a face, is there?'

'Well, look.'

Ben looked. She was right, too. He recognised it now she pointed it out. He had hardly glanced at the photograph before, just stuffed it in his pocket.

There was the pram, with its wheels sticking in the air, a sea of black mud, with the stream running through it, and beyond that a line of trees.

One tree had a sort of hump at one side. A man was standing there, his white face gleaming like a splash of paint in the greyness of the trees.

You couldn't see all of his face because of the thick black beard.

Ben sat very still.

'Well?' Isobel insisted.

'Just a fellow,' Ben muttered.

'Friend of yours?'

'Never said a word to him.'

Isobel pounced. 'Where's your camera?'

Ben was so startled that he told her. She was not sympathetic.

'You need looking after,' she told him.

No thanks, Ben thought to himself. 'Anything else to eat?'

'There's some cake in the tin, but you're only allowed a two inch slice.'

Ben conveniently discovered that he didn't know how much an inch was and cut himself a large fistful. Isobel's eyes narrowed but she didn't object.

'I bet it's still there,' she said.

'Not after I've eaten it.'

'The camera, of course. Just where you left it, I expect.'

Ben was beginning to wonder about that. He thought he'd looked; certainly, he was sure of the camera's absence at the time. Just by his sandals, so he couldn't have missed it. Or could he? Well, there was all the afternoon to find out. He'd have to rescue the raft sometime, and that was half way to the mill. It wouldn't take him more than half an hour to go and have a look. He was proud of that camera: he wanted it back.

He took another long look at the photograph. Even though it was badly out of focus, he'd know that face anywhere. A round white face with a black beard.

Ben didn't tell his sisters where he was going. It wasn't often that he took them with him on his expeditions in any case. This morning had been an exception, because he wanted to show off his raft and his skill at steering. Not too successful, that experiment, he reflected, and he was not going to ask them again.

The sun still shone as he half ran, half walked along the bank of the stream in the direction of the mill. The water had returned to its usual level now, and he could see the gravel at the bottom and the weeds waving slightly in the current. Little fish

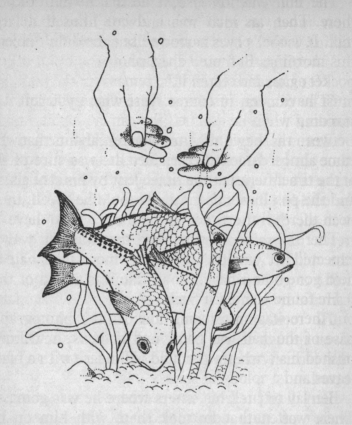

darted about in drilled ranks, like soldiers. He tried to catch some in his hands, but they were too fast for him.

He passed the place where the raft hung on its rope. The banks were high here, slippery, and steep. He could haul it up when he came back, he decided. It was safer where it was for the moment: you would hardly notice it unless you stood right at the lip of the bank, or unless you tripped over the rope.

The mill was lonely and deserted when he got there. That was what he had always liked about the mill. It was *his* place; nobody else ever came. Except this morning. Ben pulled the photograph out of his pocket again and studied the remains of the pond. It must have been just over there that the man was standing when he'd aimed the camera at the pram. Between those two tall trees where the undergrowth came almost up to the edge. Ben hadn't noticed him at the time: his attention had been fixed on the pram and the possibility of salvaging the wheels, but he'd been there all the same. The camera did not lie.

There was no sign of him now, nor had Ben expected it. Some passing tramp, that was all. Well, he'd gone now, and that was all to the good.

He found the place where he had put his sandals, but there was no camera. One of the boards at the base of the wall had gone, and he knelt down and pushed his arm into the hole. All he found was dry leaves and a colony of snails.

Ben lay on his front and peered into the darkness. There was quite a space under the floorboards, he discovered, enough to lie flat in, if you didn't mind the company. Rats probably. Perhaps a hedgehog. He could see the hole in the floorboards where the machinery had once been, the hole which he himself had enlarged that morning. There was a sort of grey light that percolated through from the big square room above.

But no camera.

Ben sighed. He hadn't expected to find it, but it would have made things easier. Isobel was bound to

39

let it out to his mother, and she'd be cross because it had been a present and he really ought to have looked after it with more care. That's what they'd say.

He got up, brushed bits of grass off his jeans and looked round the clearing. If the camera had been kicked into the mud, it would have sunk without trace by now. But he knew *he* had not kicked it. So who had?

One last look round the building. Nothing. A quick glance inside. Nothing.

Ben sat on the edge of the ragged hole in the middle of the floor and swung his legs. Well, he'd tried, and he'd have to give it up. There was still the raft.

He pushed himself to his feet and ambled towards the door.

And there it was. Just to one side of the door-frame. He hadn't noticed it when he came in. Something to do with the bright sunshine outside and the gloom inside, he supposed. He snatched it up, recognised it, inspected it.

It certainly looked all right. A bit of mud on one side, but nothing broken, not that he could see. Well, there was one sure way of finding out. He stood in the middle of the clearing and aimed the camera at the mill. It wasn't a particularly beautiful view, but it would do. But when he operated the button which produced the instant photograph, nothing happened. It didn't take him long to realise why. No film.

All right, he told himself. He might have put the

camera just inside the door instead of by his sandals as he thought, but he certainly had not used all the film. So who had?

Ben began to dislike that black-bearded tramp. He didn't mind tricks being played on him, if that was what it was, but film cost money, and he never had enough of that.

He was still furious about it when he retraced his steps downstream to the place where the raft had been tied. With his luck, he thought, that too would be gone. But it was still there. He dragged it to the top of the bank and wondered what to do next. If he'd had the pram wheels, he could have rolled it home with ease, but he had not thought that far ahead. Nothing for it but to pull.

He was hot and sweaty when he got it home. He pushed it into the shed and then went into the kitchen to splash water over his face. His mother was there, home from work. He told her about the raft, though he didn't mention falling in the water. From the look in her eye, he thought she probably guessed – and if she'd guessed, there was no point in telling her, was there?

After tea they all squashed into the mini which their mother drove. It was a regular event on a Tuesday night to visit her sister and brother-in-law who lived ten miles away on a farm. Ben always liked going: he spent most of the time in the stables. If he was lucky, he got a ride. One day, he hoped, he might have a horse of his own. But finding enough money – that was always the problem in their family.

It was late when they got back. As his mother put

the car away in the battered wooden garage at the side of the house, Ben went round to get the backdoor key from its usual place. He didn't need a light: he knew exactly where to put his hand.

No key.

Isobel, standing beside him, grumbled and pushed him away, sure that he wasn't really trying. But she couldn't find it either.

Jane said suddenly: 'You needn't bother. The door's open. The key's in the lock.'

Ben swung round. 'Hey!' he said. 'There's a light on upstairs. Burglars!'

Chapter Five

Ben raced inside. He had no idea what he expected to find: he was just angry that his home had been broken into. In any case, the light upstairs came from his room, and he knew that it had not been switched on when they all left earlier in the evening.

It was dark in the kitchen, but he knew where the furniture was. A certain amount of pale light filtered through the window from the moon, and that was enough for him. He heard Isobel behind him shouting something, but he took no notice.

The door into the corridor which ran right through the house was open. Ben ran for the staircase at the far end. A light flashed on in the kitchen, but he hardly needed that. He took the stairs two at a time, made a lightning turn at the landing, and rushed like a raging bull for the narrow staircase which led to the attics and his own room. It was *his* room which somebody was mucking about in.

Blood pounded in his ears. Light streamed from the door at the top – *his* door – and hit him like a fist in the face. He shouted. The light disappeared.

Ben tripped on the top stair, stumbled, fell flat. His head knocked the doorpost and bright stars filled his brain. Noise roared into his head like an express train, overwhelming his senses, blotting out everything else. Footsteps drummed and clattered on bare boards.

He tried to move, to get up, but his muscles refused to do what he wanted. Ben was overcome by a feeling of his own weakness. All he could do was to lie there and let it happen, however hard he tried.

Something thudded into his ribs, and he gasped, rolled, twisted away from the pounding feet. He caught a glimpse of a white face. The noise roared away down the staircase and ended with the slam of the front door.

Silence, shocking and unbelievable.

Ben pulled his knees towards his chest; he was surprised to find that he could. Slowly he dragged himself to his feet. There was no need to hurry. Whoever it was had gone now. The only thought in Ben's mind was to see whether his collection of postcards was still there. He knew that it wasn't really valuable, but it was his own.

He put up a hand to the light switch and flooded the room with a blaze which hurt his eyes. He stood in the doorway, puzzled, even frightened by what he saw.

A movement behind him made him spin round, but it was only Jane. Her eyes were wide.

'What's going on?'

Ben gestured wearily at the wreckage. 'Somebody's been giving it a going over.'

'Who?'

'How should I know?' Ben took three steps to the bed and collapsed on the edge, his shoulders hunched. His postcard collection was kept in a box

under the bed, but he didn't dare feel for it just at the moment. Not while Jane was there. If it had gone, he knew he might burst into tears.

Jane went to the door and called downstairs. Ben took a chance. His foot, searching under the bed, found the edge of the cardboard box, and relief flooded into his body. It was still there. In a second he was down on his hands and knees, making sure.

'Ben! Are you all right? Isobel said something silly about burglars.' His mother had come in. Her voice was more irritated than apprehensive. 'And Ben, really! You must tidy this room. It's a mess.'

'Somebody's been in,' Ben muttered. 'It isn't my fault.'

'Have they taken anything?'

'Not that I can see. Mum, did you see him? Old Blackbeard?'

'There was a lot of noise and slamming of doors. I thought it was you, Ben.'

'No. The burglar was up here. He kicked me. My ribs hurt.'

His mother's practised eye passed over the hunched form on the floor. 'All right,' she said. 'You'd better come downstairs and let me look at you. You can clear up the mess tomorrow. I'll make us a hot drink.'

Ben felt better with his hands round a hot mug.

Jane, for once, was talkative. 'It's just like a programme on the telly,' she was saying. 'The place ransacked, and our hero escaping with his life. You should have pumped them full of lead, Ben.'

'Not them, *him*.'

'Don't spoil it. I never knew we had anything valuable about here. Have we, Mum? There's Isobel's ear-rings, of course. She said she got them from Woolworth's, but they might have been given to her by a secret admirer with a title. Those bits of green glass are really emeralds, aren't they, Bel?'

'Shut up,' Isobel said.

'Well, he must have been after something. Is anything missing, Mum?'

Their mother was busy at the sink, and they couldn't see her face. 'Isobel, has anything gone? I can't think what we'd have worth stealing.'

Isobel shrugged. 'If Jane comes with me, I'll go and look,' she offered.

'Scared?' Ben said.

Isobel tossed her head, but Ben noticed that she pushed Jane in front of her when she left the kitchen. Ben went on hugging his hot drink. Jane was right. The burglar must have been after something. And if it wasn't his postcard collection, then what? There wasn't much in the house to interest even the least fussy thief; the house itself didn't even *look* well off; even the telly was only an old black and white. It was an old house, rambling and in need of repair, its rooms full of odds and ends of furniture, none of which would fetch much at a sale.

So why this house? It was all by itself at the end of a lane, the nearest village being half a mile away, and the town almost two miles. It had been a farm once, but now it had only a garden at the back which merged into Ben's playground, the open country beyond.

A burglar would have to be blind not to realise that this house, despite its loneliness, was hardly worth the bother of breaking into.

That was a point. He *hadn't* broken in. He'd just got the key from the usual place, unlocked the back door, and walked straight in.

The only real solution was that the intruder had seen one of them going for the key on some previous occasion and so had known where to look. It gave Ben a creepy feeling to realise that he'd been spied on. Somebody must have been hiding in that little wood at the bottom of the garden. *His* wood. Ben was beginning to be angry. He wasn't scared any more, just irritated.

Nobody had any right to spy on him, to follow him about, to pinch his camera and the film inside it.

Ben sat very still.

Of course.

He'd been a fool. The film. Blackbeard's face peering out of the trees the other side of the mill-pond. He must have known Ben had taken a photograph; he must have suspected that his face appeared on it. That was what the intruder, Blackbeard, had been after all the time – the photograph!

Ben felt in the pocket of his jeans. Yes, the picture was still there. Safe. But for how long? He'd find a safer place for it this time.

He brought it out and laid it on the table. His mother looked round. 'What's that, Ben?'

'Just a picture.'

'Let's see.'

Reluctantly Ben pushed it across the table. 'It's an old pram I found in the mud up by the mill,' he explained.

His mother peered at the little square of thin card. 'H'm. You haven't got the focus right, Ben. You ought to think a bit more before you take the picture.'

Ben was relieved. She didn't seem to have noticed the pale blob of the face in the background. 'I'll just go and see if the shed's all right. OK, Mum?'

'Yes, but come straight back, Ben. Oh, and find another place for the key. We'd better change it, I suppose.'

Ben went out into the moonlit garden. Nothing stirred in the grass and the bushes, or in the line of dark trees at the bottom. If Blackbeard was after that print, Ben thought, he'd been disappointed. And that meant he'd be back. Not immediately, though, now that he knew the house was occupied. Tomorrow, perhaps? He might be still lurking somewhere in the dark, quite near, but Ben didn't think so. He had gone rushing out of the front door, and he had probably raced up the lane towards the village. He'd have a car or a motor-bike hidden somewhere along the lane, and he'd be miles away by now.

Maybe, Ben thought, he'd have a look along that lane tomorrow. It had rained heavily yesterday, and the ground was still soft. A car or a bike driven off the lane would leave marks. He'd like to know if he'd worked it out right.

The kitchen window cast squares of yellow light

on the grass. Ben moved into the middle of it and thought about the key. He could see his mother still working at the sink. He walked over to the window and felt along the bottom of the ledge. There was a hole between the bricks and the wooden frame. Just the thing, he decided. He slipped the key into its new place and stepped back.

Now for the photograph.

He looked round the dark garden. It had become very overgrown since their father had died and mother had started going out to work, but Ben liked it that way. It had once been neat and formal, now it was more like a jungle, and nobody minded where you stepped. One of the relics of the old garden was the sundial. The square of stone at the top was loose

and if you were strong enough the whole thing lifted off, revealing a hole in the stone column. Isobel and Jane didn't know about that hole – at least, he didn't think so. Certainly, nobody else would ever have known.

Ben felt his way across the jungle darkness to the sundial. The stone top scraped as he pushed and pulled and lifted. It was as much as he could do to lower it gently to the ground. The hole was dry, smaller than he had remembered, but big enough for the purpose. He folded the photograph, pushed it in, and began to struggle with the heavy stone square.

Right, he thought, when he stepped back with a sigh of satisfaction. Nobody was going to find it there. He walked back into the moonlit expanse of grass. Not a soul. Not a sound. Not even a breath of air.

Ben went back into the kitchen and bolted the door.

'Just under the window ledge,' he told his mother.

'It took you a long time to find a place.'

Ben waved an arm. 'Well . . .' he began.

'Well, nothing. You should be in bed, Ben. Off!'

Ben went.

As he lay watching the moonlight creep across the walls of his room at the top of the house, he thought he could hear the telephone being used. Odd, he thought sleepily. Probably his mother phoning the police about the burglary. Not that anything had been burgled. Old Blackbeard wasn't as thick as that . . .

It was quite by chance that they heard the news

next morning. It was almost time for his mother to leave when Ben appeared for breakfast. The radio was tuned to the local station, and a newsreader was chattering in the background.

'Wake up, Ben,' his mother told him.

'I am awake.'

'I shall be back early today. Right? About four.'

'All right, Mum.'

'Don't get into trouble.'

'Course not.'

'I rang the police last night, so someone might be round, though I doubt it.'

Isobel was wading through a bowl of cornflakes. 'They've got better things to do,' she remarked.

'Than what?'

'Our little burglary. There was a big one at Cheap Manor last night. Didn't you hear?'

'No,' Ben said. 'What happened?'

'It's famous for its silver. Don't you know anything, Ben? Well, it's all gone. They said so on the news just now. The whole lot. It couldn't have been the same burglar as we had, could it?'

Ben said nothing, but there was no doubt in his mind.

Chapter Six

Ben's mother always said that she knew when he was up to something. He had a certain look in his eye, she said. She was looking at him now with a sort of wondering anxiety. It was time that she got out the car and drove into the town, but she hesitated at the back door.

'What are you doing today, Ben?'

'Haven't thought yet, Mum.'

'Well, think. And don't get into trouble.'

'Course not.'

'And Isobel, see that he behaves himself.' That, she knew, was the wrong thing to say, almost an invitation to Ben to commit some silliness or other. Even Isobel looked surprised.

'Anyway, don't forget to eat.'

'I won't.'

As soon as their mother had gone, Ben slipped away. Not straight out of the back door – that would have been asking for Isobel's interfering questions. He went upstairs, muttering about clearing up, for that was one thing he had been told to do, but when he got there he made no attempt to tidy anything except by kicking a few odds and ends under the bed. It would have to be done sometime, but not now.

He was convinced that he was right about Blackbeard the burglar. He'd tried to get hold of the photograph Ben had taken because he didn't want anyone to know he was in the area just before he broke into Cheap Manor. That made sense. Well, the picture was safe enough now. Ben had assumed that Blackbeard had transport, a car, or van, or a motor-bike – he'd need something to carry Cheap Manor's silver away. He must have parked it up the lane last night. Ben wanted to make sure that this theory was right. But he did not want Jane or Isobel getting in his way.

It was easy, really. He had done it before, and as long as nobody chopped down the tree, he'd do it again. His window looked out over the side of the house. Beneath his window was a low pitched roof partly covered by an enormous oak tree. There was one branch in particular which looked as though it had grown with no other purpose than to give him a good grip as he crawled over the slates. It wasn't doing his jeans much good, but Ben didn't care about that.

In a moment he was in the protecting arms of the tree, and from there to the ground was a steady climb which caused him no difficulty. He stood at the base of the trunk in the shadow of the wall, listening for his sisters' voices, but he expected that they were still in the kitchen at the back of the house, and he could hear nothing.

So far so good. The next part of his escape was through the bushes and a hole in the hedge into the lane. No trouble.

Ben walked up the lane, keeping his eyes open for

any marks of a parked car. A ditch ran along one side, and a motor-bike could have been easily hidden in it, but Ben thought Blackbeard would need something bigger than a bike. He wouldn't have left a van actually in the lane, because it was too narrow and it would be asking for trouble if anyone else came down. He'd have to get it off the road and onto the grass verge, and this lane didn't have much of a verge, except where gates led into the fields on either side or where recognised passing-places had been made. It wasn't often that anyone used the parking places because the lane led nowhere except to Ben's home, but the milkman occasionally pulled up for a quick cigarette halfway through his round at one particular gate-way.

He was there now, small and hairy and almost asleep. A newspaper was spread over the steering column of the float, and a cigarette hung from the man's lower lip.

'Morning,' Ben said.

The milkman came to with a start. 'You're out early,' he remarked.

'Looking for a van.'

'You lost one?'

'No, but it might have been parked along the side. See anything, Joe?'

Joe shrugged, folded his newspaper, threw the cigarette stub into the road where Ben obligingly stepped on it. 'Not a thing.'

Ben had hardly expected it. He was looking for marks, not the van itself. Joe got his float moving and rattled away down the lane, leaving Ben to inspect the place where the float had been. Two sets of marks, clear in the damp grass. Nothing else.

Well, there were plenty more places to look at. Ben walked on.

He found it eventually, though it took him half an hour. He had walked over a mile and was on his way back, when he came to a spot which he had already examined but not carefully enough. It was a gateway, set back from the road, leaving a triangle of short grass at the entrance. Ben climbed onto the gate to rest his feet, and it was not until he was sitting on top of it and looking down that he saw the marks, faint but unmistakable.

Two sets of wheels, a few inches wide, backing into the gate-way, then off again at a different angle. Where the van or car had stood, the marks were a little deeper, cutting into the spongy earth beneath the grass.

Ben sat where he was, considering. It might be anyone's car, of course, though very little traffic came down this lane. The milkman, the postman, the man who read the electricity meter. His mother's mini. Somebody out for a quiet drive and a look at the countryside. Well, it could be, but he was prepared to put his money on Blackbeard.

Ben looked again at the marks. A pity, he thought, that it was grass, not dried mud. He might have taken a photograph of the prints and recognised the car from its tyres – except that he hadn't got any film.

Ben never bothered too much about remote possibilities. His eyes searched the triangle of damp grass.

Weeds.

Dandelions.

Tall grass at the edges.

Blackberry brambles along the hedge. They'd be ripe soon.

A sheet of newspaper under the hedge, scrunched into a ball, rotten and dirty. Too old for Blackbeard to have been reading, and anyway Ben wasn't interested in what papers burglars read.

Still, he climbed off the gate, ambled to the hedge, kicked the ball of newspaper. It wasn't the only piece of litter there. Paper tends to collect under hedges. He bent down to pick up a scrap of white card and found it was a book of matches. Not a box. One of those little books with two rows of cardboard matches which you tear off as you want them. There was the name of a company on the front, but it made no immediate impression on Ben's mind. Two matches were still inside the book, bright orange in colour.

The odd thing was that the cardboard book looked new, not dirty like the other bits of litter.

Ben picked at one of the matches, struck it on the rough strip at the bottom of the book, watched the flame sparkle and flare until it burned down to his fingers.

That was odd, too. It had rained heavily the day before yesterday, and if this match book had been lying there then it would have been soaked and the match certainly would not have burned like that. It was a bit damp, perhaps, as you'd expect if it had been out all night, but not enough to stop it igniting.

Joe the milkman smoked, of course, but Ben knew the sort of matches he used. They came out of a box the size of half a loaf of bread which he kept on the seat beside him. Joe used to joke about it. Nobody, he said, would run off with a box as big as that.

It was a long shot, maybe, but Ben was prepared to guess that this match book had belonged to Blackbeard. He looked again at the name on the front: a hotel, that's what it was. That orange match was quite distinctive, though. Ben pushed the book into his pocket. It might be a lead. Worth hanging on to.

He began to amble back towards the house. What was he going to do with the rest of the morning? Not go home, that was for sure. Isobel and Jane would get him tidying or cleaning windows or something else that didn't need doing. He thought of the mill and wondered whether the mud at the bottom of the pond had dried enough to walk on yet. There might be all sorts of things worth having in that mud.

Ben turned off into a field. A small herd of cows looked at him enquiringly, but he skirted round them and made for the stream. He could hear it already, chattering quietly to itself within its high clay walls. He found a convenient tree to lean his back against and watched the water. It was all very tame now, after yesterday's raging flood.

He was startled by a sudden movement on the other bank, and a voice which said 'Hello'. Ben looked up quickly and saw an old man sitting ten yards further downstream. He had untidy long hair and a thin grey beard. Ben had seen him before, many times. An old tramp known locally as St Michael, because he was always calling down the blessings of Heaven on anyone likely to give him a few pence. Ben rather liked the old man: he lived his own life, and so did Ben.

'Morning,' he said.

'And another fine one. Not like the day before yesterday.'

'You must have got wet,' Ben said.

'Not I. Michael knows a thing or two, and a place where he can find shelter.'

'Oh? Where?'

'You know the mill?'

'I was just going there.'

'Well, it is open to all, though it is more like a city every day. People.'

'I'm only one.'

'Not just you,' St Michael said. His eyes twink-

led. 'I've seen you there, though I doubt you saw me. Nobody does. I make sure of that.'

Ben had a sudden idea.

'Has anyone else been around there?'

'Sure there has. Yesterday early it was. A great fellow with a bushy black beard.'

'What was he doing?'

'Just wandering and poking around. The way you do. I thought he might be a friend of yours.'

'No way.'

The old man's eyes twinkled again. 'Like me, is that it? You don't like company.'

'What did he look like?'

'Och, I took not much notice. Brown clothes, a white town face, and this black beard. I kept out of his way.'

Ben thought. It wasn't difficult to recognise the description. He pulled himself to his feet. 'Cheerio,' he said.

'The blessing of St Michael be upon you,' the tramp said, raising a hand.

Ben walked on upstream. Well, he hadn't learned much. He already knew that Blackbeard had been at the mill yesterday morning. What had he been doing? It was nowhere near Cheap Manor. Perhaps that was the reason? A burglar needed somewhere to hide his loot before he could dispose of it properly. Somewhere lonely and deserted.

Well, it was an idea. It would explain why he had been so anxious to get hold of that photograph. It could identify not only him, but also the place he had chosen to hide his stolen property in.

Ben found himself almost running.

What did that much silver look like? Candlesticks, he supposed. And silver plates and cups and jewelry. All bright and shining.

He *was* running now.

The mill-pond was still dank and sticky, but Ben was no longer interested in that. He stopped for a moment when he came to the clearing, listening to the blood pounding in his chest. There was nobody about. No sound, except for the quiet running of the stream.

Ben moved over the rough grass to the black hole where the mill door had been. The grass swished against his legs and he slowed his pace, fearful of the sounds of his own progress. When he reached the doorway, he stopped again.

What did he expect to find? Great heaps of silver over the floor? He told himself not to be a fool. Blackbeard might be a burglar, but he wouldn't be as thick as that. Slowly he pushed his head round the edge.

Nothing but a grey dimness and a bare dirty floor with a ragged hole in the middle. He walked carefully across the floor and peered into the blackness below the broken floorboards. Nothing but a faint shimmer of filtered light on damp earth.

It was then that he heard the soft passing of someone's feet through the long grass outside.

Chapter Seven

For ten appalled seconds, Ben stood as still as stone. The swish of grass had stopped. Had he imagined it? Or was it simply a rustle of wind?

No, it had been feet that made the noise which scared him into stillness. That same sound came again. Ben waited no longer. He had no idea who it was, walking through the grass softly and cautiously. It might be St Michael, or Blackbeard, or even Isobel and Jane. There was only one thing in his mind, and that was not to be seen before he could himself see who the intruder was.

With no sound he moved a step to the edge of the hole and dropped to the earth below. It was damp and soft, and it smelled of decay, but it was safer than standing in the middle of that great barn of a place, waiting to be caught like a fly in a spider's web. He crawled under the shelter of the floorboards and lay still, hardly daring to breathe.

Quiet footfalls sounded on the boards above his head. If he had wanted, he could have put up a hand and touched those boards. The space where he lay, staring into the gloom, was no more than a couple of feet high.

The footsteps stopped. Ben wished he could dig a hole in the soft earth and crawl into it, but he knew that he must make no movement. His ears were alert to every tiny fragment of sound.

A little scrape.

It puzzled him, until his nose recognised the scent of tobacco. Whoever it was up there, he had struck a match to light a cigarette. St Michael never smoked, nor did Isobel and Jane. Ben would have liked to see the colour of the match, to compare it with the book he had found by the gateway where Blackbeard's car or van had been parked. St Michael had said he had seen Blackbeard poking about at the mill yesterday. Now he was back again. Why?

A tiny scrap of thick card fell close to his head. The spent match. Ben wanted desperately to crawl to it and pick it up, but to do so would bring him into the jagged circle of dim light which came through the hole in the floor. He could hear the man's breath as he pulled on the cigarette and exhaled. Ben waited.

The man seemed in no hurry. Five minutes passed like as many hours, and still Ben lay with his face buried in the damp earth and his fingers clawing at dead leaves.

There was a thump immediately above his head, as though something weighty had been lowered to the floor. Two more footsteps, and the scrape of hands on wood. One leg appeared at the edge of the hole, dangling in space, then the other.

Ben had to go on looking. He could not move, he could not blink. He stared fascinated at those two brown-covered legs and the heavy leather boots. The man was sitting on the edge of the hole. Any second now he would drop down as Ben had done. And then Ben would be caught.

Panic thumped in his chest like a steam-hammer, and Ben was sure the man must hear it. He longed to get away, to make a dash for it, but he knew he would stand no chance.

A heavy dragging sound, and a grunt from the man whose legs dangled almost within Ben's reach. Then something solid dropped to the black earth. All Ben's muscles tensed.

It was not the man who landed beside him but a suitcase, dark, worn, and secured with a leather strap. One of the brown-covered legs pushed the case further under cover so that it almost touched Ben's face, but still he dared not move.

The two legs touched the earth, shifted, shuffled, kicked the case against Ben's head. Ben closed his eyes. He could hear the man's breathing and the rustle of the brown corduroy trousers; the scrape of his boots on the leaves, coming ever nearer.

Then all sound ceased. Had he been seen? Had the man bent down to see what was stopping the case moving? Ben held his breath until he thought his lungs would burst.

More scraping.

Grunts and a low whistle.

Footsteps.

Footsteps on the boards above Ben's head. Ben let go of the air in his chest with a quiet gasp of relief. He had not been seen. The man was going away. He had dropped the case in a safe place, and now he was off. Ben could have laughed aloud.

He forced himself to wait until every noise above his head had stopped, and then to go on waiting for another long painful five minutes while his muscles ached and the damp spread through his clothes. He could hear the murmuring of the stream by the mill-pond, clear and cool and peaceful, like a tune which ran in his head and would never stop.

He thought about the worn case. He didn't have to inspect it, or look inside it. Ben knew. Who else would drop a suitcase into this dark hole beneath the mill, except the man who had been looking for a hiding place yesterday, the man who had been afraid that a photograph would betray him, the man who had burgled Cheap Manor?

Slowly Ben began to move. His muscles creaked and complained, but he forced them to work. Low, on hands and knees, he crept out of the shadow of the case towards the light which filtered through the broken boards.

He was afraid of the light. Blackbeard might still be there, waiting for him at the doorway of the mill. Ben changed direction, kept to the shadows, moved, still slowly, round the light from the hole above his head. He would make for the side of the mill where the great wheel had once turned but now would never turn again. It was going to take him time, but he had plenty of that.

The mill wheel was stuck fast in the mud, and had been for many years. Weeds and bushes covered the places where the thick wooden paddles were missing, concealing the rotting axle which used to connect with the machinery inside, and grew all along the base of the mill where the pond once had been. Green light, dim and mysterious, showed where the edge of the building lay, and it was for this line that Ben made his snail-like way. He had tried to move without noise, but he knew that he had not completely succeeded, and this was some comfort to him and sent his former panic flying because, if Blackbeard was still in the mill, he would have heard those stealthy noises under the floor and come running to protect his loot.

But there had been no pursuit, no shout, no patter of footsteps.

Ben came to the line of bushes and waited. Pale yellow growths spread along the earth, shoots from the bushes looking for light and not finding it. The leaves were wet, for the sun had not yet reached this side of the mill. Carefully he began to part the twigs and branches, just enough to allow him a fair view of the pond and the trees beyond. The stream twinkled and glittered, and a little breeze shook the leaves into whispering motion, but there was no tall figure standing still and wary among the tree trunks, no white face staring over a black beard.

He looked to both sides. On his left he could see the line of the mill and the sudden brightness of sunlight, but on his right the great wheel rose black and forbidding, and he could not see beyond it.

Well, he reflected, he couldn't stay here all day. The case under the floor was safe enough. Blackbeard wasn't likely to move it in the light: he'd surely wait till the darkness of night covered his return.

And Ben was hungry. It must be nearly midday, and he still had half an hour's walk before he could claim whatever it was Isobel was preparing to put on the table. For the moment Blackbeard was no longer his first concern. Quickly and noisily he pushed his way out of the bushes, saying 'Ouch' when a thorn caught his hand, squeezed along the wall where the wheel stuck out, and walked jauntily into the clearing beyond.

As he thought, not a soul about. All that fuss for nothing.

He set off to run home. His first few paces were across the mud at the edge of the pond. The crust was fragile, and his shoes sank into the ooze beneath, but he took no notice. He needed food, and there was no other thought in his head. He didn't look back to see the trail he was leaving behind him.

Nor did it occur to him until he pushed open the kitchen door that he was filthy. Jane was already at the table with a book propped up against a sauce bottle. She gave him one quick look and then collapsed into laughter.

'Isobel!' she called out. 'There's a stranger come to dinner. He's black, too.'

'Very funny,' Ben muttered. 'Do you have to?'

Isobel came into the kitchen with a carton of eggs. 'I'm going to make omelettes,' she began, and then she saw Ben. Fortunately, Ben was near enough to catch the eggs as they flew out of Isobel's hands.

'Whatever have you been doing?' she demanded, and Ben thought she sounded just like his mother.

'All right, all *right*, Bel. I'll go and clean up.'

'And change. You're covered in mud.'

'OK. Give me a chance.' Ben escaped.

It was just as well, he reflected, that they'd put yesterday's jeans in the airing cupboard, because he hadn't got any more. They felt a bit damp here and there, but he'd have to put up with that. He went to the bathroom and looked at himself. Yes, he could see what they'd got excited about. He remembered pushing his face into damp earth when old Blackbeard was operating just two feet above him, and it had not improved his appearance. He peeled off his shirt and pushed his head into the basin. When he had given himself a good towelling, he felt better. He was prepared for anything when he went back to the kitchen.

'Well?' Isobel demanded.

'It's a good omelette, Bel. Thanks.'

'Don't change the subject. How did you get like that?'

'Like what?'

'All black. And if you think I'm going to wash that other pair of jeans and that filthy shirt, well, you've got another think coming.'

'Don't bother. I'll do it.'

'Huh! Where did you put them?'

'If you're not going to wash them, why do you want to know? And you can keep out of my room.'

'I wouldn't dream of going there,' Isobel told him. 'You can do it down here as soon as you've finished wolfing that omelette, otherwise Mum will find out.'

The threat was clear enough, and Ben did as he was told. When he was hanging his clothes out on the line to dry, Isobel tried again.

'What are you doing this afternoon, Ben?'

'Mending the raft.'

'Do you want any help?'

'Nope.'

Isobel looked disappointed, but she said no more about it, and that, Ben thought, was dangerous. All afternoon, while he was working on the raft, he expected her to come out and ask questions. He could hear her voice from inside, and once Jane came out, looked at him, sniffed, and went away again.

Ben had found another oil drum of about the right size, and was busy attaching it firmly to the main platform. Getting it back to the stream was easy now that he had the two pairs of pram wheels. He trundled the strange contraption down the lane and across the fields. Ben had never cared much what other people thought, and in any case, so far as he could see, there was nobody about to take much interest.

When he came to the stream, he untied the raft and slid down the steep clay banks to the water. Little bubbles came from the new oil drum and Ben swore. He had carefully chosen a drum with a big lid, like an enormous paint tin, but obviously it was not air tight. He had to haul the whole raft out of the stream, empty the water out of the drum, and batter the lid down with half a brick, before he was satisfied. Then he began to punt upstream.

It was a long quiet sunny afternoon, and Ben was enjoying himself. He knew what he was going to do, and he was pleased with the idea. It took an hour to arrive at the mill, but he made it eventually, and he fastened the raft to the bank by means of the pole. He had kept his eyes open when he came within a short distance of the mill, but there had been no movement to disturb the dusty silence of the clearing.

Ben skirted the mud of the pond and made for the doorway. It didn't take him long to drop down through the hole in the middle of the floor, drag the case out and push it over the lip of the hole.

He tried the catches, when he had removed the strap, and though they were locked, they yielded to a bit of force applied with a screwdriver which he had thought to bring with him. Inside the case was a sack, and it was heavy. Ben didn't waste time looking. He found some loose bricks lying in the grass of the clearing and packed them inside the case; then he replaced the strap and tried to batter the catches back into shape. Anyone with a torch would soon spot that something was wrong, but if his calculations were right, Blackbeard would not be back until it was dark, and with any luck he would be in a hurry. Anyway, Ben thought, he couldn't think of everything.

He dragged the heavy sack down to the raft, eased the front oil drum out of the water, and loosened the lid. He had guessed right about the size. The sack and its contents fitted nicely inside and still left room for the lid to be replaced. The raft might have lost some of its buoyancy, but it had certainly gained in value.

He was about to set off downstream when he

remembered the screwdriver. He last recalled seeing it on the floor by the hole, and he couldn't leave it there for Blackbeard to fall over. Anyway, it was a good screwdriver. He hurried back to the mill.

It was dark inside. The sun had gone down beyond the line of trees, and a cool evening breeze was beginning to stir the branches. Leaves scraped and rustled.

He found the screwdriver, pushed it into a pocket, and ran back to the door. Somehow the mill seemed creepy and hostile in this dim light.

He had not reached the door when his blood froze and his muscles tightened into useless knots. A long searing scream split the silence of the clearing, like a wolf howling at the moon.

Chapter Eight

Ben's mind was an empty blank. If only he knew what had made that noise, he might have known what action to take. There were no wolves in England, except in zoos, and no other animals that he knew which could make that blood-freezing howl. Again it came, low and menacing, then rising to a devilish scream full of pain and loneliness.

The noise brought Ben to his senses. He sprang for the side of the door and the shadows of the walls, trying to make himself invisible in the gloom. His hands scrabbled at the rough surface for a weapon, but all he did was scrape his nails. He pulled the screwdriver out of his pocket: it wasn't much, but it was better than nothing. He gripped the blade and raised the wooden handle in front of his face.

Another long low shriek, nearer, more piercing.

Ben grasped the iron blade until his fingers ached.

A shadow, short and vaguely familiar, fell across the doorway.

'Ben!'

The screwdriver clattered to the floor.

'Ben!' It was Jane's voice which rang inside his head, and suddenly he was furious. He dashed out of the cover of the wall, into the square of light which was the doorway, stood there, his eyes sparking with anger and his fists clenched.

'What the *hell* are you doing?'

'Language,' Jane reproved him. 'We thought you'd be here. Are you all right, Ben? You look all white.'

'Course I'm all right. Was that you? That row?'

Jane looked amused. 'Quite good, wasn't it? I was practising my Brownie howls, and Isobel didn't like it at home. She said I'd break the windows. But I could hardly do that here, could I?'

By all the harps in Heaven, Ben thought, remembering a phrase he'd once heard St Michael use – *Brownies!* He knew that Jane had strange tastes, and that once every week she went off dressed up in brown, but did she have to bring her loathsome habits here?

'It's Brownie night tonight,' Isobel said. She was sitting on a pile of bricks a few yards away. 'I told her not to, but she would do it.'

Ben rescued the screwdriver: he couldn't trust himself to speak. He had been scared, and it was all Jane's fault. Slowly he straightened, and saw that Jane was holding out a paper bag.

'It's getting late,' she remarked. 'Tea time. We brought you some cake.'

Ben collapsed on the doorstep and laughed. It was chocolate cake, his favourite, and he sat there and ate it while his mind returned to normal.

'Well, you might say thank you,' Jane remarked. 'We've come a long way.'

'I'll take you back on the raft,' Ben offered.

'Thanks,' said Isobel. 'We'll walk. Come on, Jane, or you'll be late for your meeting.' She got up and began to walk away.

'Thanks for the cake,' Ben mumbled. 'Any more?'

'Yes. At home. Don't be late.' Isobel enjoyed telling him what to do, though it wasn't often that he did it.

Ben watched them go. Then he sighed. Well, it had taught him a lesson. Behind every wolf howl was a Brownie bearing cake. It was worth remembering. He went back to the raft.

He arrived home not many minutes after Isobel. Jane had already gone to her meeting, but their mother wasn't back yet. Ben made himself some toast, and, as an afterthought, some for Isobel.

'Did you get the raft back?' she asked.

Ben champed toast and thought. 'Yes,' he admitted.

'Where have you put it?'

'In a safe place.'

'In the shed,' Isobel said.

'Well, yes. And I've locked the door.'

Isobel laughed. 'That won't stop anyone. The wood's rotten.'

The trouble was, Ben thought, she was right, but he couldn't think of anywhere else. His mother certainly would not have it inside the house.

'Any more cake?'

'No, that was the last bit. I was going to make some more tonight.'

'Good,' Ben said. 'Remember I like chocolate.' He wandered out into the garden and looked at the shed. Rotting wood and rusty hinges. It wouldn't take Blackbeard more than ten seconds to get inside. But he didn't know, did he? Nobody had seen him transfer the sack from the case to the raft, Ben was sure of that. With any luck, when Blackbeard came to pick it up, he wouldn't even notice that the contents of the case were different. He'd be in a hurry to get off and away.

And he *would* get off. That, Ben thought, was all a bit tame. Blackbeard ought to be caught. Another thing: it was all very well rescuing a sackful of silver, but what was he going to *do* with it? He supposed that it would all have to go back to Cheap Manor eventually, but it seemed a pity.

Ben wondered where Blackbeard was. Hiding somewhere in the daylight hours, waiting for dusk. Well, that wouldn't be long now. There was the photograph: that was still in the hollow under the sundial. And a book of matches.

He pulled the little square of cardboard out of his pocket and looked again at the orange match, not that it told him much. He turned it over in his hands.

'Thorpe Motel.'

Ben suddenly paused in his wanderings. It was a chance, a good chance, that the words printed on the back were the clue he had been hoping for. He couldn't imagine why he hadn't thought of it before. The Thorpe Motel was not much more than a mile along the main road.

Ben raced round to the lean-to hut where he kept his bike. In a moment he was mounted and off into the lane. He could hear Isobel shouting at him from the kitchen but he took no notice. He had to draw

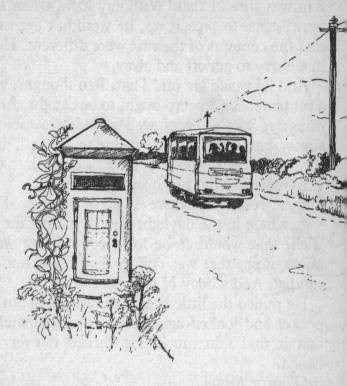

into the side of the lane once in order to let his mother's mini pass. She waved at him and he grinned back. And then a few minutes after that, a small twelve-seater bus passed him, full of small girls all dressed in brown, and a large lady in severe blue. Ben grinned again. Jane's Brownies must have some sort of expedition planned for this evening, he supposed, and it looked as though they were holding it in the fields by the stream. At least, his mother wouldn't have to wonder why he was cycling in the

opposite direction; he was just being sensible and keeping out of the way. Ben raced on.

The bike was an old one, but Ben knew how to get the best out of it. Within ten minutes he had arrived at the motel, a long range of doors and windows on two floors and a big square of a building at one end where the entrance was lit with red and yellow lights. Ben pushed his bike round the end, following the signs which pointed to the carpark. A belt of trees concealed the carpark from overlooking windows. Ben had time to draw breath and consider.

What was he looking for?

He could hardly march into the reception area and demand to see a burglar. If he gave a description without a name, he would probably find himself thrown out as a nuisance. If his theory about Blackbeard was right, however, there ought to be a van or a car belonging to him in this carpark.

Ben looked over the line of cars. Casually he walked down the back of them, his hands in his pockets, as though he was filling in time waiting for someone, as though he had every right to be there. Nothing struck him as odd or out of place. His confidence began to ebb. He turned at the last car and strolled along the front. Five cars, a closed van, and a couple of motor-bikes. The van was probably the most likely. He stared at the bonnet and the windscreen. A little red doll hung from the driver's mirror, grinning at him with cynical contempt.

He was about to give the whole thing up in disgust when he noticed something orange on the dashboard of the car next to the van. He peered through the driver's window at a book of matches lying next to a packet of cigarettes. The book was open and the matches were orange.

Excitement quickened in Ben's chest. He knew perfectly well that these books of matches must be on sale to anyone at the motel, but it was the only lead he had and he was going to stick to it, whatever happened. It would be worth noting the registration number, even if it was false.

He glanced quickly over his shoulder, expecting to see the tall figure dressed in brown and complete with shaggy black beard bearing down on him, but there was nobody in sight. What should he do? He could hardly hang around all night.

Voices broke into his thoughts and he ran for cover among the trees which lined the carpark. A party of young men and girls strolled round the corner and piled into the van, laughing and talking. The van drove away with a bump and a screech.

Ben found a bench at the back of the trees and sat down to watch. The evening sun had gone below the level of the motel roof, and he was reasonably sure that he would not be noticed, unless someone was looking for him particularly.

Time passed slowly, and Ben was bored. It was cold, just sitting still and doing nothing. His attention had wandered when he suddenly realized that someone had come round the corner and was walking quickly and silently across the tarmac. A tall figure, dressed in brown. His back was towards Ben, but he was sure the face would be half-hidden by a black beard. Ben stiffened on the seat and drew further into the shadows. He heard an engine being started and the mumur of wheels over tarmac. The car purred out of the carpark and into the main road.

Ben raced for his bike. He could just see the car disappearing round a bend as he skidded into the road. He pounded after it, but by the time he reached the bend, the car had gone.

Ben pedalled on. He knew he had no hope of

catching the car, and he wouldn't have any idea what to do if he did. All things considered, it had not been a particularly successful idea. He had better go home.

He turned into the narrow lane which led to his house. His eyes were on the road in front of him, and he almost missed the dark green car in the gateway to a field. When he *did* see it, he jumped on his brakes and nearly fell off.

The car was empty, but the number plate proved it to be the one Blackbeard had been driving.

Ben cautiously looked round. Blackbeard must have gone over the field to follow the stream to the ruined mill. At any rate, he was nowhere in sight. Ben smiled grimly and reached into his pocket for

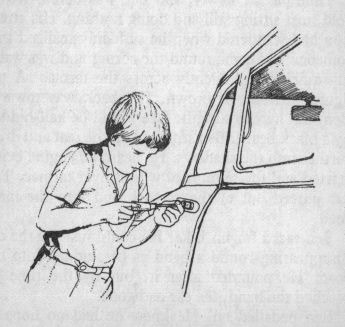

the screwdriver. He could do some useful work with that.

It was a few minutes afterwards, when the job was done, that he smelt burning and saw flames leaping up under a cloud of thick black smoke.

Chapter Nine

A red living heart in a dark green field, and a dozen small brown creatures writhing about it. Little screams and excited laughter. A deep female voice issuing orders and organizing confusion.

Ben watched from the roadway. It was the field next to the house, and it had been invaded by Jane and her Brownies. She had probably mentioned, although Ben could not remember it, that her group was going to have a bonfire and barbecue that evening, and here they all were, having fun. There was a smell of smoke and sausages, and for a moment Ben was envious. Then he skirted the field and made for the stream.

Jane saw him and came running over.

'Ben, where are you going?'

'Just out. Have fun.'

'We're cooking, and then we're eating.'

'I knew that.'

'You could have some, if you liked. Mrs Hammer wouldn't mind.'

Ben was tempted, but he had more important things to do. 'Thanks, Jane. I'll be back. You lot staying long?'

'Till it's dark.'

Ben strolled away, trying not to look as though he was in a hurry. The bank of the stream was a golden line of light in the evening sun. The water babbled cheerfully. There was no sign of Blackbeard. He must be nearly at the mill by now, Ben thought. Was it worth giving chase? He'd left his bike in the ditch down the lane. He began to run.

Suddenly he came upon St Michael, the white-haired tramp. He had a bundle of newspapers by his side, and he was sitting with his back against a tree, watching the sunset.

'Good day to you,' he said, 'and the blessing of Heaven. As usual.' His blue eyes twinkled, and his thin hair waved in the breeze. He was wearing a tattered overcoat and a dirty scarf. Ben had never seen him without them.

'Seen anybody?' Ben asked, as though he had nothing better to do than to chatter to tramps.

'Now who would you be after? There's a party of elves playing with fire in the field back there.'

'Not them. They're just Brownies.'

'And I thought they were the little people. Life is full of disappointment.'

'Nice evening,' Ben said. 'Anyone else about?'

'No. Nobody that you wouldn't know.' The tramp's canny eyes looked at him sideways.

'A man?'

'Indeed.'

'With a black beard?'

'He might be said to have that ornament.'

'And he went upstream?'

'That very way.'

'About a quarter of an hour ago?'

The old man moved his thin shoulders. Time meant very little to him.

Ben suddenly decided to take a chance. An idea had come jumping into his head, but he needed St Michael's help. He sat on the grass by the old man and talked.

'He's a burglar, and he's got the loot he took from Cheap Manor last night hidden away in the mill. At least, he thinks it's there, but it isn't, because I've put it somewhere else. Safe. He's gone to collect it, and he'll be coming back this way because his car's in the lane.'

'And won't he know the silver's gone?'

'He might, and he might not. Anyway, I don't want him to get away. I thought if we could lure him to the house, we could lock him up in the cellar.'

'Just you?'

'Well, I'd need a bit of help. That's where you come in.'

'Oh?'

'You see, he knows the house. He was there last night, looking for a photograph I took which had his face in the background.'

'And has he got it?'

'No. I've hidden that under the sundial.'

'So?'

'If you tell him that the photograph is in the cellar, he'll go there, and I can close the trapdoor on him. Simple.'

The old man nodded. 'The holy saints save us,' he said.

'You'll do it?'

'Sure I will. An entertaining evening it will be.'

Ben scrambled to his feet. He was feeling like a

general disposing his forces before a battle. Excitement flickered in his eyes.

'Thanks, St Michael.'

Ben ran back to the lane. The Brownies were still there, but he took no notice of them. There was one more thing he had to fix, just to make sure he didn't lose his man, and he had to do it fast. He had seen his mother driving home. She would be there now, cooking or cleaning or doing something useless. Ben didn't want her in the house when Blackbeard arrived. She'd only get in the way and make objections.

She looked surprised when Ben burst into the kitchen. Mrs Hammer wanted her, Ben said, at once. To help with the Brownies. Was Jane hurt, then? Of course not. Jane never came to any harm. It was just that Mrs Hammer needed another pair of hands.

Ben's mother put on a pair of stout shoes. 'Remember to lock up,' she told him over her shoulder as she went. 'Isobel's out.'

'Sure,' Ben said. But he made no attempt to reach for the key under the ledge of the kitchen window. He ran back into the house to check the bolts on the trapdoor which gave entry from the corridor beyond the kitchen to the cellar. There was nothing in the cellar except a pile of coal, a ladder, and a large colony of spiders. Blackbeard would be company for them.

He suddenly thought of the cellar's outside entrance through which a delivery of coal was shot to the pile below. Ben ran outside and pushed his way through the scrubby growth which almost concealed it. One bolt looked a bit loose, but the other was firm enough. It ought to hold the prisoner safe. It didn't occur to him to wonder what he was going to do with Blackbeard when he'd caught him. He'd think of that when it happened.

All he knew now was that he did not have much time. Blackbeard would be on his way back now, with the case. Just about at this moment he'd be talking to St Michael. Would he take the hint? Ben began to have doubts. He couldn't just sit around waiting and biting his nails. He wanted to *know*.

He ran back into the lane, meaning to skirt round the edge of the field where the Brownies were burning their fingers on hot sausages and baked potatoes, and so to the stream. Then he thought of the path, and how exposed it was. He'd be seen as soon as Blackbeard came, and Blackbeard knew his face.

The raft. Of course. He could paddle silently upstream, concealed under the cover of the willows and the tall steep banks. He just had time to launch it if he hurried.

Again the pram wheels proved their worth. Without them, it would have been a long haul over rough grass to the stream, but with them the trip took no more than a few minutes. He had lowered the raft to the water, and had turned back to hide the wheels in the bushes, when he heard the sound of someone pushing through undergrowth.

His first fearful thought was that he'd left it too late, and that Blackbeard had spotted him. But

Blackbeard would never have said in tones of such clear satisfaction, 'Ben, Mum's cross.'

Isobel.

'I'm busy,' Ben told her shortly.

'Doing what?'

'Minding my own business. Why don't you do the same?'

Isobel was not offended. She was used to Ben. 'Why did you send Mum to the Brownies?' she demanded.

Ben muttered something unintelligible. He had to get Isobel out of the way, and it looked as though she was happy to stay there chattering all night.

'Clear off,' he said.

'Shan't,' Isobel replied calmly. 'Why, Ben?'

'Because I thought she'd like it.'

'You're up to something.'

'No.' Why didn't she just *go*? 'You go and have a sausage, Bel.'

'Later.'

'They'll all be gone if you don't hurry. You know what Jane's like with food.'

'And you, Ben. I know you're up to no good, or you'd be over there by the fire, cadging.'

'Huh!' Ben slid down the bank to the raft and grasped the pole.

'Where are you going, Ben?'

'Shan't be long.'

'That's not what I asked.'

'Timbuktoo,' Ben said desperately. 'Go *on*, Isobel. I've got things to do.' His insistence served only to confirm Isobel's suspicions.

'Can I come for the ride?'

'You'll only fall in again. And you didn't like it last time.'

'You need looking after,' she said, in that motherly tone of voice which Ben always resented.

'Shan't be long, Bel,' Ben said again. He pushed the pole into the mud and edged the raft into the middle of the stream. Maybe she'd take the hint if he just went. The trouble was that Blackbeard couldn't be far away, and he didn't like the way Isobel was calling out to him, shouting in order to cover the increasing distance between her and the raft. She was even following him, pushing her way through the trees and bushes on the lip of the stream. She'd give him away, sure as fate. The noise she was making was enough to frighten a deaf elephant.

'Wait for me, Ben!'

Ben groaned. He'd thought out his plans so carefully, and now they were all going wrong because Isobel was being dense, as usual.

'Mum will want you to help with the Brownies,' he suggested desperately.

'What?'

Ben repeated his remark, a little louder.

'Oh no, she won't. She was going to stay there with Mrs Hammer, but they didn't want me.'

'Nor do I,' Ben muttered. It was one good thing, however, that his mother had decided to keep out of the way. He punted hard, feeling the strain of the current against the oil drums, particularly the one at the back with less room in it for air. The water bubbled and chattered. So did Isobel.

90

'Somebody's coming,' she remarked.

Ben's senses jumped. Blackbeard! He pulled the raft into the cover of an overhanging willow and flattened himself against the thick trunk. A slithering noise above him brought his heart into his mouth, but it was only Isobel. She landed on the raft in a heap.

'Who was it?' Ben whispered.

'Big fellow. Brown trousers. Black beard. I didn't like the look of him.' She crouched by his side under the tree.

Footsteps, firm and confident, crunching on loose gravel and swishing through grass.

Footsteps, nearer and louder.

Footsteps, right above their heads.

Chapter Ten

Ben and Isobel looked at each other with wide scared eyes. Surely the man on the path above them must see the raft, and wonder, and investigate? And if he did, they had no chance. Ben felt a sudden panicky desire to run for it, to break cover and race off as fast as he had ever gone in his life, but he knew that their only hope lay in total silence. The raft rocked gently beneath his feet, and the water lapped and gurgled.

The man was whistling, not loudly, but as though he was pleased with himself. Was it Ben's imagination? Or was one leg meeting the ground with a heavier thud than the other? He'd have the suitcase with him, weighing him down, and if he was pleased, that would mean he had noticed nothing odd about the locks. He would be making for the car now, with a quick visit to the house to pick up the photograph – if St Michael had done what Ben asked.

The footsteps and the whistling passed by, and Ben breathed again. He even dared to look up and peer through the hanging branches of the willow at the man's retreating back. Yes, he had the suitcase.

Ben gripped Isobel's arm and whispered to her not to make a sound. Then slowly, steadily, he began to push the raft out into the stream. He didn't

want to lose Blackbeard, and so long as Isobel didn't talk, this was the quickest and easiest method of pursuit. The gurgle of the current covered any noise he might make with the pole. In the distance he could hear the shrieks and squawls coming from Jane and her Brownies. The raft slid silently downstream under the cover of the weeping willows.

They were not far from the point where the bridge had collapsed and formed a dam. Ben steered the raft into the sticky mud at the edge of the river. He could see the tangled mass of the timber which the water had swept down and then abandoned in a little bay. The thought crossed his mind that one day he could use those planks.

Isobel began to clamber up the steep bank. Ben was pleased to see that she was trying to do it quietly; she'd learned something, after all. He hooked one arm round a branch, fitted one foot into a hollow above a flint, and hauled himself up. If Blackbeard was making straight for the car in the lane, he ought still to be in sight. Ben peered round the trunk of the tree, and was satisfied when he could see no one. Blackbeard must have cut across the field towards the back of the house. You could see the chimney pots from this part of the path, and it was an easy three minutes' walk. Probably he had heard the Brownies at their devilish practices and thought it wise to leave the stream before he reached the field in which they were making life full for Mrs Hammer.

Ben knew this country. He could go anywhere within five miles of his home and be certain of not being seen unless he wanted. Each ditch and bank and copse was a known friend. If he and Isobel marched straight across the field towards the house, they'd stick out like an elephant in a window-box. But there was a hedge surrounding the field, and just beyond it a ditch. Sometimes there was water in it, black and better left undisturbed; there would probably be some now, after the rains of two days ago. He'd have to risk that. He glanced at Isobel and saw that she was looking clean and neat and tidy. Well, some things were more important.

She did not object when he explained in a hurried whisper what he meant to do. It crossed his mind that probably she didn't believe him, but that it might be better to keep him under her eye and out of mischief.

They reached the hedge and slipped down in the ditch. It was wet, but only with the occasional puddle. It was certainly easier than crawling along the edge of the field with bent backs so that their heads did not show above the bushes.

When they came to the back of the garden, Ben paused. There was plenty of cover here, and he wanted to be sure that the garden was unoccupied before he ventured along the side where the sundial stood. There were a few metres of open ground which could be seen from the kitchen window, but after that they'd be safe.

Ben surveyed the windows and the back door. The evening sun slanted in and made the glass glitter and shimmer. It was impossible to tell whether anyone was inside watching. But Blackbeard would not suspect he was being followed. He might well think that the house was occupied, but once he discovered that it was not, he'd be inside like a rocket and searching for the cellar, anxious to find the photograph and be out again as soon as he could. All he would find was a heap of coal, but that ought to keep him busy for a bit.

Ben and Isobel ran lightly along the line of the hedge until they reached the sundial. For a moment Ben wondered whether Blackbeard had realised that the photograph was hidden in the hollow of the stone, but the sundial was firm and didn't look as though it had been disturbed. There had been no shout, no sudden rush of movement as they crossed the open ground. Ben felt safe.

Hastily he whispered instructions to Isobel. She was to stay outside and keep out of the way. Ben had no thought of protecting Isobel from possible danger: he considered merely that she'd be a nuisance inside. He was surprised when she nodded agreement.

Ben padded to the back door. It was very slightly ajar, and he stopped for a second in thought. Perhaps his mother had left the door unlocked? Then he remembered that he himself had been the last to leave the house, and he was reasonably sure that he had shut the door. It didn't matter very much. The important thing was that Blackbeard was inside.

Ben put his ear to the crack, but he could hear nothing from the kitchen. Gradually he eased the door open, just enough for him to slide through, and stood motionless on the mat.

There were noises now. Noises of things being moved and thrown about. Ben grinned. Blackbeard was down among the coal. Calmly and without hurry, Ben glided round the big kitchen table to the door which led to the passage. It was closed, but he knew how to open it without noise. The passage opened before him, dark and warm and comforting. Ben moved to the place where the trapdoor stood leaning against the wall. The noises from below sounded thunderous now. Blackbeard clearly was interested not in how much row he made, but only in how fast he could find what he was after and be away. So much, thought Ben, to the good.

The hinges of the trapdoor, he knew, squeaked. He began to ease the thick square of wooden boards away from the wall. The hinges screamed, and there was a sudden ghostly silence. Ben's heart thudded. His fingers seemed glued to the wood, and his feet to the floor. If Blackbeard's head appeared through the trap, he knew that he would be incapable of movement.

The beam of a torch shot out from somewhere below, lighting up the square hole and the tall figure in the middle of the cellar. Still Ben could not move, fascinated by the light which spun and tumbled and glowed. Then the light went out, leaving a darkness as black as the pit and as soft as velvet.

Something faint and white and evil floated in the middle of the square hole. Blackbeard stood immediately beneath and was looking up. The faint white circle of his face moved, and the black line of his body lunged towards the fixed ladder which led to the passage above. He had climbed three steps, and the white circle had almost reached the surface when Ben let out a yell, a cry half of fear, half of triumph. His muscles leapt into action. The square of the trapdoor banged into place. Ben fumbled desperately for the great black iron bolt. It wasn't used much, and it was sticking. Ben was kneeling on the trapdoor, tugging at the bolt, unaware that he had torn a nail and that his finger was bleeding. He could feel the trapdoor beginning to move beneath him, and he jumped and landed again with all his force, and again bent to the bolt.

It moved. With a screech and scrape it moved and slid into the ring, and Ben leaned back on his heels, fighting for breath.

Slowly he picked himself up. He'd done it. His head was full of his own daring, and it did not occur to him that he had no idea what to do next. He had captured Blackbeard, and that was enough for the moment.

Strange that there was no noise from below.

There had been one thump, and that was all. Blackbeard must have realised that the bolt was strong; perhaps he had broken his shoulder when he tried to break through. Whatever it was he was doing down there, Ben felt secure. He was tired. And happy. He had Blackbeard trapped!

Ben went into the kitchen, walked unsteadily to the sink, and ducked his head under the cold tap. Then, with his eyes full of water, he groped for the towel. He felt better after that. He sat on the doorsill and looked at the setting sun. The sounds of

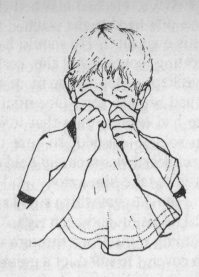

laughter and excitement were audible from the Brownies' field. Ben almost convinced himself that he could smell the sausages. Just the thought of them made his mouth water and his throat contract.

For the moment, however, he hadn't the energy to get up and walk to the field. The sun was warm on his face, and like a cat he sat there and enjoyed it.

At first he didn't understand the noise which erupted all round him like an unexpected roll of thunder. Then, after he had sat there for what seemed like hours, as though paralysed in a cast of plaster, he was up and running. The noise had come from the side of the house, and it was the noise of splintering wood.

As he rounded the corner he had a vision of what he was going to see. There would be Blackbeard, towering over him, and behind that tall grubby figure the broken remains of the shoot through which coal was delivered to the cellar.

It was all his own fault. He should have remembered the rotting cover over the coal shoot. It wouldn't have kept a dog in for more than fifteen seconds. He had been so sure. One brief look at the cover, and he had been certain that it would hold. He had been so self-satisfied, so sure that he had won, that Blackbeard was securely held until someone else arrived to take him away.

Ben crept to the dustbin which stood at the corner of the house. His vision had been right. Blackbeard was there, hauling himself up through the remains of the broken cover. He stood for a moment with his back to Ben, and as he turned, Ben ducked back behind the bin.

Things happened so quickly after that, that Ben had no time to think, or decide, or act. The brown-dressed figure rushed past him, to the back of the house and the garden beyond, making for the line of trees and the field which led to the stream. Ben had time to notice the marks of the coal on his face, his hands, his clothes, and at any other moment he would have laughed, but not now.

The brown figure dashed and leapt away, following the high hedge at the side of the garden, and when he was half-way down he came to a sudden and immediate stop. Ben rose from behind the dustbin. A yell of warning stuck unuttered in his throat. He had forgotten Isobel.

She was still there, by the sundial, just where Ben had told her to stay. She stood, firm and unyielding, barring Blackbeard's path, with pale set face and arms uplifted. As Blackbeard began again to run, swerving past her, she put out a foot and brought him crashing to the ground. His arms flailed, and he rolled against the sundial till it rocked and swayed and almost fell. Then he was up, and his hands went to the sundial for support. He took two steps, limping; stopped, sought again the help of the sundial which tottered under his weight. The top stone fell with a dull thump to the grass. Blackbeard stared at the column which was left, sticking up like a broken tooth. His hand went to the hole revealed by the fall of the stone from the top, and he uttered a cry of victory mingled with a hacking laugh as he saw what he held in his hand. Then he was running, fast and silent and sure, to the cover of the trees.

Ben saw him bend to pick up something square and heavy from behind a tree, and then he had gone. He had the suitcase and the photograph, and there was no further reason for him to linger.

Chapter Eleven

Ben was angry. He had planned Blackbeard's capture, and his plans had gone wrong. It was his own fault, he knew, but that did nothing to calm him down. He was going to get Blackbeard if it was the last thing he did.

He shouted to Isobel, and she, for once taking orders without question, ran to the front of the house and the lane. She was making for the Brownies' field, but she never reached it. Blackbeard suddenly appeared at the hedge, still dragging his heavy suitcase, and she screamed at him. He dodged back from the hedge, running across the field to the far corner where there was a gate into the lane. Ben pounded after him. He was not trying to conceal his presence any more. He was out in the open, and so was his quarry. Running was the only thing in his mind now. Just keep running, he told himself. One foot in front of the other. Nothing else mattered.

Blackbeard had reached the gate, but so had Isobel. She appeared like an animated scarecrow in the gap and waved her arms at him. He veered again to follow the hedge, and Ben changed direction too. It did not occur to him where they were going. His only concern was to keep up with the tall figure ahead of him, and he knew that the distance between them was increasing. Blackbeard, despite the suitcase, was a good runner.

Suddenly he had disappeared. Ben came to a thudding halt. A man doesn't just vanish into thin air, he said to himself. Hedge, line of trees, open meadow – where was he? Ben's eyes flickered round in an effort to locate the object of his pursuit. Not a sign of him. Ben's spirits dropped. He'd lost him, after all.

His ears caught a curious slithering and sliding noise, and abruptly everything fell into place. He knew that noise. It was the result of dragging something heavy across the steep slope of the bank of the stream. Beyond that line of trees water gurgled and splashed. Blackbeard had taken to the water.

Ben broke into a run, across the tussocks of grass to the gloom of the trees. As he ran, he tried to think what part of the stream Blackbeard was making for, and then it came to him with a sickening thud of realisation that just beyond that big willow was the raft.

When he burst from the trees on to the path, Blackbeard was already fifty yards downstream, standing firmly on the raft and using Ben's pole to fend off from the banks. Ben watched for a second in hopeless anguish. He'd never catch him now. And to add to it all, Blackbeard was getting away with the *real* silver concealed in the oil drum.

A map of the stream sprang into Ben's mind. It wound in a series of bends and curves round this field and the next one until it met the lane. But Ben could get there first if he cut across the field, and if he started now.

His muscles ached, but he took no notice. He took a great lungful of air and raced away. Another thought sprang into his mind. He had a picture of a little bay in his head, a broad curve in the stream-bank, and a mass of tangled planks, the remains of the collapsed bridge. That particular spot was just a few yards beyond the next big clump of trees. He forced his way through the brambles and under-growth, slithered down into the bay and began to tug at the great planks.

The first one he launched into the current turned head-on and floated uselessly downstream, but the second caught a tree root and stayed. Water bub-bled round and over it, but it stuck firm. Ben dragged out another plank and began to build. Not a dam – he didn't have time for that – but just enough obstruction to make Blackbeard leave the raft and return to land. Then maybe, if Isobel succeeded in doing what he had told her, they'd have him.

One more plank, and then another. Ben glanced up, saw the raft just rounding the bend, and sprang back behind the rest of the timber, crouching down and trying hard to be invisible.

Blackbeard saw the obstruction, jumped for the bank opposite and began to pull himself up the tall bank. He threw the suitcase up, then clawed with hands and feet at the soft clay until he stood at the top. Without a backward glance he picked up the case and was off. The lane was no more than a hundred yards away, and he'd be there in less than half a minute.

Ben rose from his concealment. He was half-way across the stream, using the planks he had thrown in as a bridge, wading the rest of the way, when he noticed the raft. It sat firm and level in the water. Ben's heart sank. The raft should have been lower one end than the other, but it wasn't. He paused long enough to glance at the oil-drums. The drum in which he had hidden the sack of silver was without its lid.

So Blackbeard had known all the time. Blackbeard had taken the silver, and even now must be reaching the safety of the lane and his car. Ben smiled grimly. Well, he'd see about that.

He made for the corner of the field where he knew the gate led to the lane just beyond where Blackbeard's car was parked. The hedge was high just there, and he could watch the lane without being immediately noticed. He gave a quick glance up and down the lane to see that everything was ready. Isobel had done her part. 'Good old Bel!' he muttered to himself, and withdrew into the shadows of the hedge.

It was grey in the lane. The setting sun had dipped below the trees, and a cool wind played round his wet jeans, but he knew he had not long to wait.

Footsteps. Firm and hasty. Blackbeard making for the car and not caring that his feet kicked stones which rolled and spun and rattled.

Ben waited.

Round the corner of the lane he came, tall and brown and hurrying. The case dragged at his arm, and he dropped it by the side of the car as he put his hand in a pocket for the keys. Something bright glittered in his fingers.

Still Ben waited and watched.

Through the cover of the bushes he could see Blackbeard's face, see the look of disbelief, hear his snort of anger. Blackbeard loped to the other side of the car, tried that door, then with increasing desperation the two back doors. Nothing stirred except Blackbeard's quick steps and his glittering eyes.

Ben grinned to himself. A screwdriver forced into a car's keyhole and twisted can make a lock useless. For once, he thought, something had gone right.

Time for the second part of his plan.

Blackbeard had now realised that the car was useless to him, he had picked up the case, and was already beginning to run down the lane.

It was then that Ben rose from his hiding-place with an ear-splitting yell which made Blackbeard spin round in his tracks. Ben raced out, round the car, straight at his legs. Blackbeard swung the heavy case, and Ben found himself knocked sideways, reeling to the ground. One thought whirled round his head: they ought to be *here*, he heard himself saying. Were they all deaf?

Then he saw Isobel. She had a set fixed look on her face and she was coming down the lane from the house at a gallop, waving a great stick in her hand and shouting for all she was worth. Behind her, racing and yelling and shrieking, came a small company of figures dressed in brown. One of them still had a half-eaten sausage in her hand, but the rest were armed with sticks and bars and lumps of wood.

Blackbeard saw them at the same time. He turned, half-fell, picked himself up. Ben could see the look of desperation in his eyes as the yelling mob closed in. Blackbeard ran.

Round the bend ahead of him appeared more brown figures. The hedges were alive with them and the lane was full. Jane was at their head as they charged towards the car and its owner. Blackbeard saw them, gave a terrified glance over his shoulder, saw Isobel's army, made for the narrow grass verge. Perhaps he had some idea of bursting through the hedge and escaping that way. He did not see Ben.

Ben had by now recovered his wits, though his head was still full of stars and whirling circles. He had pulled himself to his knees when he saw Blackbeard coming straight at him. He put out an arm to fend off the advancing figure, but Blackbeard still hadn't spotted him. Ben's arms were suddenly full of flying feet and kicking legs. He held on with all his strength, and Blackbeard fell. Ben's world became a cavern of darkness.

He could hear the pounding of feet and the yelling of high voices. He kicked out with his feet, found something solid to push against, began to crawl. Just in time. The two armies of shrieking Brownies met on top of Blackbeard, and they pummelled him and sat on him like so many hungry sparrows diving on a crust of bread, until there was no more fight in him.

Wearily Ben got to his feet.

'You OK?' Isobel said, matter-of-factly.

'Sure. It went well, didn't it?'

'Course.'

A deeper voice of authority broke into the excited chatter of the Brownies. Mrs Hammer had tried to restrain the marching of the armies, but when they followed Jane and Isobel, she had no alternative but to come as well. She had taken a longer time to cover the distance, being large rather than speedy, but she had made it at last, like a tank covering rough country.

'Whatever are you doing?' she demanded. 'Girls!'

She looked again at her group of Brownies. 'Good heavens!' she said, shocked. 'You've caught a man!'

'He's a burglar,' Ben said.

'Get up at once!' Mrs Hammer ordered.

'I don't think he can,' Ben's mother remarked. She was standing beside Mrs Hammer, and, Ben noticed, looking amused. 'Not while they're all sitting on him.'

Jane looked up quickly. 'He's safe now. We've tied his hands behind his back, and we've put a rope round his ankles.'

'I bet it's a granny knot,' Ben muttered. Jane ignored him.

Ben moved stiffly to the case which lay on the grass, and began to undo the straps.

'I think,' his mother remarked, 'that I'd better call the police, don't you, Mrs Hammer? We can hardly leave the poor soul here all night.'

Ben sat back on his heels. The case was open in front of him, and he was looking at the bricks and lumps of wood with which he himself had packed it. No silver.

'It's not at the mill, and it's not in the raft,' he mumbled to himself, 'and it's not here, so where on earth is it?'

Somehow, Blackbeard without his silver loot had lost all interest for him. The silver had gone, and the sunshine with it. A dim greyness settled over the lane and over Ben's spirits.

'The blessing of Heaven,' remarked a cheerful voice above him. Startled, Ben looked up and saw St Michael's grey hair and wrinkled face through the hedge. The old man moved out of the cover of the bushes and leaned over the five-barred gate. His tattered old coat hung loosely from his thin shoulders, but there was enough light left to bring the twinkle to his faded blue eyes.

'Were you looking for something?' he enquired. 'I see you've found your friend.'

'The silver,' Ben wailed. 'It's gone.'

The old man chuckled. 'There's not much St Michael doesn't see along the stream,' he said. 'Is it not in the drum under your raft?'

'No,' said Ben. How did St Michael know about the raft?

'No, of course it wouldn't be, would it? Not after I'd rescued it. Not at all a safe place, I said to myself, when I saw you put it in. Would this be what you were looking for?'

Part of the shapeless old coat separated and became a sack. St Michael swung it from his shoulder and dropped it over the gate at Ben's feet.

'That's it!' Ben shouted. 'Thanks, St Michael!'

'Not at all,' said the old man. He began to move away towards the path along the stream, though he was still talking as he went. 'You'll find it all there. Well, most of it. Just a little souvenir for myself, you know. The blessing of Heaven.' His shambling figure was lost in the gathering darkness.

Ben did not complain. In his opinion, St Michael deserved his little souvenir.

THE SHORE

David St. John

THE SHORE

Houghton Mifflin Company Boston 1980

Library of Congress Cataloging in Publication Data
St. John, David, date
The shore.
I.   Title.
PS3569.A4536S5   813'.54   80–14018
ISBN 0–395–29473–8
ISBN 0–395–29474–6 pbk.

Printed in the United States of America

V 10 9 8 7 6 5 4 3 2 1

The poems in this collection first appeared in the
following magazines: *American Poetry Review:*
"Portrait, 1949." *Antaeus:* "Song Without
Forgiveness." *The New Yorker:* "The Shore,"
"Blue Waves," "Guitar," "Hotel Sierra," "Until
the Sea Is Dead." *The Paris Review:* "Of the
Remembered." *Parnassus:* "The Olive Grove."
Poetry: "The Avenues," "Elegy," "The Boathouse."
Some of these poems also appeared in the limited
edition, *The Olive Grove,* published by W. D.
Hoffstadt & Sons.

Section V of "Of the Remembered" is for Howard
Norman. "Until the Sea Is Dead" is for Beth.

I would like to thank the National Endowment for
the Arts and the Guggenheim Memorial Foundation
for fellowships in poetry, which aided in the
completion of this book.

for my mother and father

We might hurt each other if we were together, but apart, we should be hurt much more, and to less purpose.

SIDNEY KEYES,
in a letter

CONTENTS

1   THE SHORE

4   BLUE WAVES

6   THE AVENUES

8   GUITAR

9   OF THE REMEMBERED

28 ELEGY

31 THE BOATHOUSE

33 HOTEL SIERRA

37 SONG WITHOUT FORGIVENESS

38 PORTRAIT, 1949

41 THE OLIVE GROVE

43 UNTIL THE SEA IS DEAD

THE SHORE

THE SHORE

So the tide forgets, as morning
Grows too far delivered, as the bowls
Of rock and wood run dry.
What is left seems pearled and lit,
As those cases
Of the museum stood lit
With milk jade, rows of opaque vases
Streaked with orange and yellow smoke.
You found a lavender boat, a single
Figure poling upstream, baskets
Of pale fish wedged between his legs.
Today, the debris of winter
Stands stacked against the walls,
The coils of kelp lie scattered
Across the floor. The oil fire
Smokes. You turn down the lantern
Hung on its nail. Outside,
The boats aligned like sentinels.
Here beside the blue depot, walking
The pier, you can see the way
The shore
Approximates the dream, how distances
Repeat their deaths
Above these tables and panes of water —
As climbing the hills above
The harbor, up to the lupine drifting
Among the lichen-masked pines,

The night is pocked with lamps lit
On every boat off shore,
Galleries of floating stars. Below,
On its narrow tracks shelved
Into the cliff's face,
The train begins its slide down
To the warehouses by the harbor. Loaded
With diesel, coal, paychecks, whiskey,
Bedsheets, slabs of ice — for the fish,
For the men. You lean on my arm,
As once
I watched you lean at the window;
The bookstalls below stretched a mile
To the quay, the afternoon crowd
Picking over the novels and histories.
You walked out as you walked out last
Night, onto the stone porch. Dusk
Reddened the walls, the winds sliced
Off the reefs. The vines of the gourds
Shook on their lattice. You talked
About that night you stood
Behind the black pane of the French
Window, watching my father read some long
Passage
Of a famous voyager's book. You hated
That voice filling the room,
Its light. So tonight we make a soft

Parenthesis upon the sand's black bed.
In that dream we share, there is
One shore, where we look out upon nothing
And the sea our whole lives;
Until turning from those waves, we find
One shore, where we look out upon nothing
And the earth our whole lives.
Where what is left between shore and sky
Is traced in the vague wake of
(The stars, the sandpipers whistling)
What we forgive. *If you wake soon, wake me.*

BLUE WAVES

I think sometimes
I am afraid, walking out with you
Into the redwoods by the bay. Over
Cioppino in a fisherman's café, we
Talk about the past, the time
You left me nothing but your rugs;
How I went off to that cabin
High in the Pacific cliffs — overlooking
Coves, a driftwood beach, sea otters.
Some mornings, over coffee, we sit
And watch the sun break between factory
Smokestacks. It is cold,
Only the birds and diesels are starting
To sound. When we are alone
In this equation of pleasure and light,
The day waking, I remember more
Plainly those nights you left a husband,
And I a son. Still, as the clouds
Search their aqua and grey
Skies, I want only to watch you leaning
Back in the cane chair, the Navaho
Blanket slipping, the red falls
Of your hair rocking as you keep time
To the machinery gears, buses
Braking to a slide, a shudder of trains.
If I remember you framed by an
Open window, considering the coleus

You've drawn; or, with your four or five
Beliefs, stubborn and angry, shoving
Me out the door of the Chevy; or, if some
Day or night
You take that suitcase packed under
The bed and leave once again, I will look
Back across this room, as I look now, to you
Holding a thin flame to the furnace,
The gasp of heat rising as you rise;
To these mornings, islands —
The balance of the promise with what lasts.

THE AVENUES

Some nights when you're off
Painting in your studio above the laundromat,
I get bored about two or three A.M.
And go out walking down one of the avenues
Until I can see along some desolate sidestreet
The glare of an all-night cafeteria.
I sit at the counter,
In front of those glass racks with the long,
Narrow mirrors tilted above them like every
French bedroom you've ever read
About. I stare at all those lonely pies,
Homely wedges lifted
From their moons. The charred crusts and limp
Meringues reflected so shamelessly —
Their shapely fruits and creams all spilling
From the flat pyramids, the isosceles spokes
Of dough. This late at night,
So few souls left
In the place, even the cheesecake
Looks a little blue. With my sour coffee,
I wander back out, past a sullen boy
In leather beneath the whining neon,
Along those streets we used to walk at night,
Those endless shops of spells: the love philtres
And lotions, 20th century voodoo. Once,
Over your bath, I poured
One called *Mystery of the Spies,*

Orange powders sizzling all around your hips.
Tonight, I'll drink alone as these streets haze
To a pale grey. I know you're out somewhere —
Walking the avenues, shadowboxing the rising
Smoke as the trucks leave their alleys and loading
Chutes — looking for breakfast, or a little peace.

GUITAR

I have always loved the word *guitar*.

I have no memories of my father on the patio
At dusk, strumming a Spanish tune,
Or my mother draped in that fawn wicker chair
Polishing her flute;
I have no memories of your song, distant Sister
Heart, of those steel strings sliding
All night through the speaker of the car radio
Between Tucumcari and Oklahoma City, Oklahoma.
Though I've never believed those stories
Of gypsy cascades, stolen horses, castanets,
And stars, of Airstream trailers and good fortune,
Though I never met Charlie Christian, though
I've danced the floors of cold longshoremen's halls,
Though I've waited with the overcoats at the rear
Of concerts for lute, mandolin, and two guitars —
More than the music I love scaling its woven
Stairways, more than the swirling chocolate of wood

I have always loved the word *guitar*.

OF THE REMEMBERED

I

I will tell you. Maybe
You're leaning in the open
Doorway of some Irish bar,
Watching a single tug
Edge a little clumsily into its
Slip, in a Baltimore twilight;
Maybe we're driving the bluffs
Of New Mexico one Sunday morning,
Or maybe the coffee's just
Starting to boil
In the bare kitchen of your rickety
House by the Pacific, as every
Circular pulse of the lighthouse
Slices the dawn fog. Maybe,
At midnight, high on the catwalk
Of the abandoned cannery, we'll
Watch the bent
Ghost drag his skiff onto the shore,
Turning its keel to face the partial
Moon. Maybe it's this drifting in time
You'll no longer imagine, or the body
Of my voice that you hate. Tell me —
Because you remember a woman calling
Out in our sleep? Because nothing's
Left, if
We're alone? *Tell me*. I will tell you.

II

I grew up in California,
Where everyone stood a little closer
To the sun. In the San Joaquin
Valley, where I lived, the orchards
And vineyards ran from the Coast Range
To the Sierra foothills;
Those low barracks in the fields went
Politely ignored until the harvest;
Those months of winter fog,
Just the simple revenge of every swamp
Drained off for farm land. Summers,
To escape, I drove to the mountains
Or west to the Pacific, where the beaches
Sprouted heavy eggs of tar as
The off-shore wells
Broke down. In spring, the Sierra streams
Flushed and cleared with melting snows;
I'd sit by a falls, picking watercress.
Once, I watched a dazed squirrel
Drop from a high pine onto a rock
Below. At the tree's base
I dug a shallow bowl in the dirt,
And wrapped the squirrel's split face
In the thick robe of its tail. Late
That summer, I walked
Blue Canyon with a friend, along the trail

His great-grandfather had first broken.
We sat on the slanted porch
Of the loggers' company mess hall; inside,
Cast-iron stoves with grills as wide
As beds, still greased like obsidian. My
Friend whistled an old square-dance reel,
Stomping his boots on the broken boards,
To keep time. A year ago, one afternoon
In Big Sur, I was telling this same story
To my son as we knelt at a cliff's lip
Watching the waves ravel over the rocks.
He stopped me short, pointing to a crescent
Cove where a piece of swollen driftwood
Listed in the tides. I cleared the focus
Of the binoculars onto the coarse fur
Of a seal, its corpse. Even
I tire of emblems. One night, lost
In the typical smoke and liquor
Haze of a club in Montreal, I listened as
The awkward quartet lapsed and soared close
To dawn. Nobody cared if the sax missed
Its cue from the bass,
Or if the brushes shrugged off the drums,
About those bridges the piano player found
And lost. Yet, as I imagined the words
I might hang to the melody, the sax player

Stood and held a single low note
Over the dim room. The piano player stopped,
The drummer. Then slowly the sax began again,
In that breath caught by the entire bar,
Another tune none of us could name.

III

Why, it must be close by him, at that
moment, his old home that he had hur-
riedly forsaken and never sought again,
that day when he first found the river.

 KENNETH GRAHAME,
 The Wind in the Willows

I had walked out into the meadow
Of words, utterly lost. I can remember
My mother and father waving from the towers.
A few blackberry hedges forked here
And there, dividing the meadow into its maze;
The stiff green walls printed
With buckshot, rat droppings, owl garbage —
Berries, any stain on my fingers. Yet,
I'd never imagined the succulent tongues
Others' dreams could offer. That day, such
An elegant script drew its cirrus on the sky.
I know if the child runs from every meadow,
These weirs and copses, he comes only
To the backwaters flooding the tall, erect grasses;
A surface breaking with the letters of a law . . . .
So, it is this animal sense of belonging
Which lifts your face into the folded blessings
Of the air, into this night blanketing every crib
Of cornstalks by the coiled highways. Though
We too can rise like woodsmoke

From a thin chimney in the pines, as each of our
Lost books kindles the ravings of that fire
Which bakes those dozens of chattering blackbirds
Into one very sweet and remarkable pie.

IV

I first slept along this estuary years
Ago, where the Navarro fans into the Pacific;
I was married, twenty. A few days before,
Driving out of the mountains above
Santa Cruz, I stopped at a country store
Along the way. Outside, the newsrack:
Cambodia, Kent. I drove north until I came
To this wide scallop of sand and driftwood;
I wanted to stand by the flat waves. In our
Truck, parked in a cliff hollow of pine,
My wife was singing our son to sleep
As the spray whipped up across the night,
Covering me. I've read in books
How a person might one day splinter into slivers
Or spines of light, but I only remember falling
Unconscious on the white sand. And it makes little
Sense, the noise I heard in the distance
As I came slowly back to myself, maybe just blood
Circling in my ears, or the scrub of the cliff
Set humming by the rising storm, or else
An iron dulcimer
Struck somewhere out beyond the sea. Now, this
Morning, walking again these banks of the Navarro
Towards the Pacific shore, the beach seems so calm,
So undramatic: only the limp kelp, a few driftwood
Limbs, the sand. As I walk beside the water,
I've kicked up out of nowhere

Half an old pair of dice — the wobbly Captain
Rattling the bones in his pocket, chancing it all
On the horizon. Yet this single die is so
Small, so beaten by the waves, sand, and coral
Its holes seem carved at random, its edges
Almost round. I know just where I'll use this ivory
Knuckle: I'll slip it into a game of liar's dice
As I lift the felt cup off the polished counter
In front of the solitary bartender. Then, I'll tell
This story, though the chances are
It's nothing he'd really listen to, let alone believe.

V

Here, tacked by the table
That is my desk, where I sit
In the mornings as the sun unties
The winter trees, is the photo
Of a wolf more
Beautiful than you would imagine
Standing in a landscape
Entirely snow. Caught in profile,
The wolf is turning its head
To face the brief snap of the camera,
Its coat, like the frost on my windows,
A dim shine tinged with rust. Sometimes
I sit here very late at night
With only one small lamp bent towards
The wall, its narrow bone of light barely
Touching this photo, taken in Canada
And sent without explanation by a friend,
This wolf. Never blinking, never looking away.

VI

Now   the breaths no longer freeze
Along the pane   now the light curls
In each leaded square   or page
Or Chinese screen   these characters
Drawn past   waves brushed along the silk
Chaos   detail   music or the web
The names of the world hang briefly   halos
On a broken surface   the loose hand
Shadows inking the fire-lit screen
Signature gestures   lyrics
The trespasses   the shared boundaries
The married spaces of cold news   weaving
One and two bodies nearly equal to the world
Unequal to their dream
Now say it   now   in the dialect
Of fingers over fingers   a corporeal tongue
A script of genitals   the stiff accents
Of snow on the manes of horses
The manes of young men   young women
The strokes of the stick along the tablet
The baking black clay   the scored fingers
Of stone   so now say it   word's flesh
The salts   the blame   the father's son
The triad's ghost   the crows or the rasp plea
Rainbows bent from a book to earth
The book of leaves   newly falling leaves
The corpses   veins flattened in their pages

The burning manifestoes   the diaries
The leaves like sheets floating
Over each flat body   the smoky seamy air
The ambivalent air   now say it   worshipful
Palm leaves laced with leather cords
No logic's pulse   branches at the window
Or the fire breaking its frame
Elegiac conversations   slack wastes
Of the pillow   the monologue of the double
You undress   semaphores   bodies along the bed
The broken circle   old unbroken square
Now say it   the white lotus in the fallen veins
The white cocoons   the white needle in the sun
The powdered light   catechisms
No last song rising in the closed rooms
First faith   bone tablet   the skin's shale
The blossoms in every last region of delay
These erasures   with   within these weather notes

There is a melody inventing itself

VII

Earth. The word
Mystified me as a child —
With my parents at Italian movies
I heard the truck drivers on the screen
Call the dark women at the roadside
Cafés: *earthy.* And I imagined their pulses
Circled like the sun's, with the tides
Of a daily moon. I began to watch carefully
As every leaf uncurled and waved, falling
To the earth. Plums, figs, apricots, cherries —
They all fell, splitting to seed. I paid
More attention to the rivers stroking the calm
Earth, though — finally — I forgot it all:
I lived in small rooms, piling my books against
The closed door, pouring the acrid coffee
From pot to cup. Then I met a woman
Who loved to sit in the round window of my room
Burning piñon and lemon grass, taking off
Her clothes when the talk turned abstract. Who'd
Walk me down the paths of the shore gardens
Lying through her teeth about the ancient Mayan
Dragonfly of hope. One night,
She found me in a dockside bar waiting to step
Onto the blackened oily water. The next morning,
She said nothing;
We played my warped 78 of Charlie Poole singing
Didn't He Ramble. Soon, too, I left. New Mexico,

The high plateau of Acoma, to sit on the ledges
Of the cliff face at Puye among the carved
Caves of the pueblo, where, for a while, time
Was the sun. In Yosemite, last August,
Hiking the trail to Glen Aulin with my son, I felt
That same print of day. Walking off into the trees
We'd come onto a clearing of low grass. On my back,
As the sun rose towards noon, almost asleep and
Hidden by the trees, I could hear a file
Of rented horses
Shuffling to their stables in the valley below,
And the voice of one rider cautioning — about stocks —
A friend. I opened my eyes. On his stomach, my son
Had crawled to the center of the meadow
Where a city of ground squirrels teased him, rising
First from the holes in the distance, then by one
Of the tunnels at his knees. Closing my eyes, I
Listened as the horses and voices faded, as
My son began chirping at the dozen gold phantasms;
And I slept, my back against the earth.

VIII

For one year, in both summer and winter,
Everywhere I slept I dreamed of
Women waking crying. Any season, in any bed —
Of one woman asleep beneath the iced windows
Of Our Risen Saviour Hospital. Another
Curled like a ghost crab in a leather chair.
And of those leaving husbands, lovers, sisters
In San Francisco, London, or outside Cheyenne.
Of women waking to the finches crying
In latticed geometries, in praise. Women waking
Crying, as dawn detailed the city skyline;
All the taxis off Sixth Avenue circling, circling
Like old ballads, simple lives.

IX

Twin memory, we all seek it
As some God seeks us, though we
Await a softer, more temporal
Lover. That family
We carry across our shoulders,
The coat dedicated to the unending
Winter, advises us on each mistake.
Snow covers the leaves, shadows die
Into a mutual orbit, myths burn
In their seasonal constancy. Tonight,
I remember a story I once read
Of a hero who, to begin his quest,
Must sail across the sky
To its other shore, where his father
Waits, ages dead, to teach him those
Secrets which unlock evil, pointing out
Every road radiating from our star.
Norse? Hindu? Neither, I think.
I've only taken pieces of several
To make one story I love, one chord
I hear most. My friends know it,
In those words for their dead fathers,
That long approach. One summer, as my
Own father's heart rose like a hummingbird
Into his throat,
I wanted to speak *then*, not in any
Postscript of prayers, how I'd hold his head

In my arms. Now, as the snows still brush
The trees of Baltimore, I know my father
And his curious heart are walking again
In the California sunlight, not yet knowing
This melody is his. If I drove for six
Days west, I might ask him, on that other
Shore, for those answers I'm not certain
I wish to know. Chalice of mountains,
Valley of figs and grapes, where he lives.
And though I travel randomly now, at great
Distances, perhaps those spaces we cannot
See across are less dark
Framed by the two bodies we still carry,
Each for the other. And though my own son
Knows memory pales only slightly any day
Apart, if we stand together
As my graceful father walks the steep path
Along the limestone wall at this garden's end,
Perhaps we'll both see, as I still wish to see,
If, as the stone door closes, faith follows.

X

Of the remembered
We speak like stones standing
Like any saint whose cold fingers
Hold a blunted tongue
Of the remembered
Scraping the honeycombed earth
Of the remembered
In a garden where the sunlight turns away
Of the remembered
Whose breaths hang like ash
As they recite each loop of the sparrow
Of the remembered
Whose dice roll against the door
Of the remembered
Holding square sails in either hand
Their hearts caged in smoke
Of the remembered
Rising in the cup of morning
Swinging pitchers of black wine
Of the remembered
At the gates and borders of flint
Revolving in the pupil of the tamarisk
As their boat draws on towards
The set double horizon
Of the remembered
Who tire of being talked about
Who hold still the crescent knife

The skull the prayer flags the sands
The white mandolins
Of the remembered
Who look everywhere for their luggage
At the steps of the forty-nine days
The seven black sails times
Seven leaves of night
Of the remembered
Passing the gates of nectar and toad
Of the remembered
Who are footstools dressed in our robes
With paper faces and bound feet
With conch cake silk and flowers
With mirrors and lyres colored
At the end by flame
Of the remembered
Who will be judged by these scales
Of white pebbles and black
Of the remembered
Closing the soft vertical eyelid of the door . . . .
You light the fire, lay the silver, set the table
With one plate. Behind you, the aged, leaded
Pane reflects the red speech of the liquid evening
Fire . . . . Sitting in the square
Of an old church, I watch the woman I first
Took for you — her face shadowed by the cathedral's
Ornate spire — as she works

The patched bellows of an Irish pipe. The day's bells
Begin to call past the river's scoured bridges, where
The black branches of the trees cross against the sky's
Marine, lit evenly by the slowly rising Easter sun;

Of the remembered, named . . . .
                                    A drone, reeds: *the melody.*

ELEGY

If there is any dwelling place
for the spirits of the just;
if, as the wise believe, noble souls
do not perish with the body,
rest thou in peace . . .
                    TACITUS

Who keeps the owl's breath? Whose eyes desire?
Why do the stars rhyme? Where does
The flush cargo sail? Why does the daybook close?

So sleep and do not sleep.

The opaque stroke lost across the mirror,
The clamp turned.
The polished nails begin the curl into your palms.
The opal hammock of rain falls out of its cloud.

I name you, *Gloat-of-*
The-stalks, drowse-my-embers, old-lily-bum.
No matter how well a man sucks praise in the end
He sucks earth. Go ahead, step
Out into that promised, rasp gratitude of night.

Seeds and nerves. *Seeds*

And nerves. I'll be waiting for you, in some
Obscure and clarifying light;
I will say, Look, there is a ghost ice on the land.

If the page of marble bleeds in the yellow grass,
If the moon-charts glow useless and cold,
If the grains of the lamp outlast you, as they must —
As the tide of black gloss, the marls, and nectar rise

I will understand.

Here are my gifts: *smudges of bud,*
A blame of lime. Everything you remember crowds
Away. Stubble memory,
The wallpaper peeling its leaves. Fog. Fog
In the attic; this pod of black milk. Anymore,

Only a road like August approaches.

Sometimes the drawers of the earth close;
Sometimes our stories keep on and on. So listen —

Leave no address. Fold your clothes into a little
Island. Kiss the hinges goodbye. Sand the fire. Bitch
About *time.* Hymn away this reliquary fever.

How the sun stands crossing itself in the cut glass.

How the jonquils and bare orchards fill each morning
In mist. The branches in the distance stiffen,
Again. The city of stars pales.
In my fires the cinders rise like black angels;
The trunks of the olives twist once towards the world.

Once. I will walk out into the day.

THE BOATHOUSE

All the last lessons of fatigue,
Every passage naming its reprieve —
Also, the few
Commitments of the heart. I thought
I'd pass as smoothly as a hand passes
Over a globe of light
Hanging in some roadside bar,
Or over the earth on its pedestal of oak
In a library. I believed I'd take
What came, a life with no diary's
Hieroglyphics,
Only the crooked arc of the sun.
Now, even the way I sleep speaks habit;
My body slipping into the heat,
The crumpled beds. Every voice I hear
Within my own (*of the father,
The mother*) remains a saying so
Lost to its history. Look
How I treated the day,
Waking listlessly beyond the pale
Of those horizons scored along another
Subtle back. And so trust
Seeps only into the most concrete
And simple acts: the fox coat, the slap,
The gin smashed against the window. Maybe
Homer had it right. A man sails
The long way home. Now,

Every new morning-after lights
Those medleyed veins of white wisteria
Strung
Above the door; no alibis survive. Half
Of the boathouse has collapsed, the shingled
Roof sloughing off its tiles — as
Even the sea sings one octave in the past.

HOTEL SIERRA

The November air
Has curled the new leaves
Of the spider plant, strung
From an L-bent nail
Driven in the warp of the window
Frame. Maybe the woman down
At the desk has a few more opinions —
On the dying plant, or the high
Bruised clouds of the nearing storm,
Or the best road
Along the coast this time of year
To Oregon. This morning, after
You left to photograph
The tide pools at dawn, the waves
In their black-and-white
Froth, I scavenged in your bag
For books, then picked up one
You'd thrown onto the bed, Cocteau,
Your place marked with a snapshot
Of a whale leaping clear of the spray
Tossed by the migrating
Herd — a totem
Of what you've left to dream. Yet,
It's why we've come — *Hotel Sierra* —
To this place without a past for us,
Where, I admit, a dozen years ago
I stayed a night across

The hall. I never asked why, on this
Ocean, a hotel was named for mountains
Miles inland. I spent that cold
Evening playing pinball in some dank
Arcade. Tonight, I'll take you there,
Down by the marina with no sailboats,
By the cannery's half-dozing, crippled
Piers rocking in the high tides and winds
Where I sat out on the rotted boards,
The fog barely sifting down,
The few lights
Looped over those thin, uneasy poles
Throbbing as the current came and went.
Soon, I could see only two mast lights
Blinking more and more faintly
Towards the horizon. I took
A flask of gin upstairs, just to sit
At the narrow window drinking
Until those low-slung, purposeful
Boats returned. As I
Wait here this morning, for you,
For some fragment of a final scene,
I remember how I made you touch, last
Night in the dark, those
Summer moths embossed upon the faded,
Imperial wallpaper of the room.
Now, as I watch you coming up

The brick-and-stone path to the hotel,
I can hear those loose wood shutters
Of the roof straining in the winds
As the storm closes
Over the shore. I listen as you climb
The stairs, the Nikon buzzing
Like a smoked hive
Each moment as you stop in front of:
A *stair-step; a knob of the banister;*
The worn brass "12" nailed
To our door; the ribbons: knots of paint
Peeling off the hall —
You knock open the door with one boot,
Poised, clicking off shot after
Shot as you slide into the cluttered room,
Pivoting: *me; the dull seascape hung*
Above the bed; the Bible I'd tossed
Into the sink; my hands curled on
The chair's arm; the limp spider plant . . . .
Next week, as you step out
Of the darkroom with the glossy proofs,
Those strips of tiny tableaux, the day
And we
Will have become only a few gestures
Placed out of time. But now rain
Slants beyond a black sky, the windows
Tint, opaque with reflected light;

Yet no memory is stilled, held frame
By frame, of this burlesque of you
Undressing. The odd pirouette
As your sweater comes off, at last,
Rain-soaked slacks collapsing on the floor.
Tomorrow, after we leave for good
The long story we've told of each other
So many years not a friend believes it,
After we drive along the shore to Albion
To your cabin set high above the road,
After we drag your suitcases and few boxes
Up to the redwood porch,
After the list of goodbyes and refusals ends,
We'll have nothing to promise. Before I go,
You'll describe for me again those sleek
Whales you love, the way they arc elegantly
Through water or your dreams. How, like
Us, they must travel in their own time,
Drawn simply by the seasons, by their lives.

SONG WITHOUT FORGIVENESS

You should have known. The moon
Is very slender in that city. If those
Letters I sent,
Later, filled with details of place
Or weather, specific friends, lies, hotels —
It is because I took the attitudes of
Shadow for solitude. It is because you swore
Faith stands upon a black or white square,
That the next move
Is both logical and fixed. Now, no shade
Of memory wakes where the hand upon a breast
Describes the arc of a song without forgiveness.
Everything is left for you. After the bitter
Fields you walk grow deep with sweet weeds, as
Everything you love loves nothing yet,
You will remember, days, you should have known.

PORTRAIT, 1949

Of the pain, I have nothing . . .
Even the radio lies.
The books won't remember you right.
You knew how much
Was bribe or circumstance. What to give
Or give up. They all loved you,
As only a man who quotes Lenin can afford
To be loved — out of a helplessness,
Disgust. Those good looks of a statue
Kept getting you by,
A few well-timed revolutionary fashions.
They hung posters in every
Toilet, chalked your name on the seats
Of the subway. They catalogued
Each bridge you blew, each village freed,
Every journal and clandestine poem
That sifted hand to hand
Across the country. You forgot just what
Was true. Thank God the government despised
You. That stare that said nothing,
To anyone! One eye almost closed, the other one
Closed. You were reaching up from a chair,
Leaning over to pick
The ripest grapefruit from the bowl, to turn
The first page of the morning newspaper,
To see who was lying again. The sunlight washing
Over you. The mail kept coming, whole

Sentences sliced out. "*Apologies* . . . (*or*)
Shrugs." Once, the black curls a lover clipped
And sent, along with a blank
Sheet of paper, knowing you would understand.
There's nothing so erotic as a kind
Of understanding. After all, you'd say to me,
There is only one story, but it's told many times.
Just as my story begins
With a man out scattering cornflakes for the birds,
Bread for the ducks. When it ends he is a hero.
In between, the passage grows complex,
Attentive to leather gloves, carbines, rubber hose,
Confessions. A boy's limp head on your chest.
You leave the story in a cellar
Full of long racks of meat, casks of cheese, barrels
Of summer sausage,
Bicycling down a road lined with dying blackberries,
The stars so close over your shoulder. You must
Find the church with two steeples —
Stop there. Nobody really wanted to hear;
They'd all hoped for something else. Not these words
About your journal of the winter
Farmhouse, of that woman and daughter who hid you;
How, that Christmas, you helped them carve
A whole nativity of hard, black rye!
Joseph and Mary, all the animals and Wise Men, black
Bread . . . .

All the interviewers walked away confused.
Even today, they seem confused. The radio uncoiling
Its eulogies. They should say
You were the one man who'd pin a newspaper to a bench
Staring at it, piss off a bridge and hit the train
Below. I suspect what matters
You've left hanging, it seems, you've left hanging.

THE OLIVE GROVE

Never lost in its false, dense weather
The man in the olive grove sits

Dreaming as the fog drifts
And smokes through the lattice of the branches.

There is nothing about his life
He does not know. He knows that even the split

Parings of his bones will at last gleam
In the wet earth. He knows the buckle

Of muscle will fasten his heart, as the coronas
Blaze out of their saints. But where, he thinks,

Is that blessing pale as a summer?
Where is the reaper beneath his shoulders of wheat?

The bark of the trees flakes in long curls.
The man in the olive grove crouches a moment

Beside the turned roots, their shoots
Like the hair pulled from the moon's harvest shag.

He shakes out his pockets —
Photos torn from a newspaper, a letter from

A friend blaming him, lint, a ring of keys
To a chain of rooms, phone numbers smudged into

Names, a tan cigar, matches turned to clay, clay.
What is visible at last in the dark

Leaves guttered in the road's throat? Or
Does the wind remember the last room of the valley?

He thinks *he* must not remember the business
Of a man in the olive grove, though he has never

Before lied. He told what he saw.
He was milk to everyone; the certain, pale medium

Of desire. But the heart of the window breaks —
Now, the peacocks sweep through the grove.

Someone steps out onto the path
Bowing, as if beginning a dance he does not know.

Everything is over. *Once more*. The worst is past.

UNTIL THE SEA IS DEAD

What the night prepares,
Day gives: this cool
Green weave to the light
Shading the darker emeralds
Of each branch as they descend
The narrow trunks of pine
And Douglas fir along the steep
Uneven slope of the hill,
Its jagged sockets of rock
And sudden gullies. Every amber
Bridge light fades at dawn,
A few redwoods cluster
By the pitted highway
At each bend, and, beyond,
Those white hummocks rise shagged
With ice plant and wiry scrub
Half a mile or so
Before they flatten at the sea.
There the shore cuts like a thin
Sickle at the fields
Of black waves. On a rise above
These dunes, I watch the wild oats
Leaning with the wind, as I try
To imagine what I could
Write to you beyond these few
Details of a scene, or promises
You already know. Perhaps

I'll draw myself into the landscape,
To hold you closer to it
Than I could alone. Below, the dunes
Grow dark even in this harsh
A light: the sand burns
With the same erratic white
Within a negative held up
Against the sun. These dunes —
The Dunes of Abraham — were named
For the story of a Russian
Trader who stayed
To live in the hills above Fort Ross,
Long after his fur company
And its hundred soldiers sailed home
To Alaska. In the spring
His Spanish wife left him, leaving
Also the clothes and books brought
From Madrid, and her small son,
Almost two. Late one night, he took
The boy down to the dunes
And tied him against the bent
Skeleton of an overturned skiff;
In the moonlight, the child
Shone blue and flat, like the fresco
Of a cherub painted high
Across the dome of a cathedral ceiling.
The Russian took his curved fishing

Knife, then hooked
Its point into the skin below
His chin's cleft and yanked the blade
Along the fraying vein of his
Own windpipe. At dawn, a woman driving
A drag of timbers
From the mill down to the harbor
Found the boy, alive, his skin laced
By welts where the taut ropes
Webbed his body. In towns along
The coast, they said
It was a miracle the way God
Had turned the hand of Abraham away
From the son, against the father. Some
Nights, in the pockets of these dunes,
A gull or bat will sweep up
In an ashen light, startled by the whisk
Of my pants in the stiff grass;
I'll stop until the urgent flapping
Dies, until both the body
And its shadow enter the fog beginning
Its nightly burning of the shore.
As the horns sound, a beacon
From the jetty skims the vague sands
Of the reefs. From here,
I can see the husk of the De Soto
Someone pushed, last summer, off the cliff.

If I'm tired, sometimes
I'll sit awhile in its back seat —
In the mixed scent of salt, dead mollusks,
Moldering leather, and rust. The rear axle
Caught on the last low rocks
Of the cliff, the hood nosed dead-on
Into the tentative waves of a high tide,
The odd angle of the car,
Make it seem at any moment the rocks
Might give way, sending me adrift.
And I know I'll bring you here,
If only to let you
Face those dreams you woke me from
One night as the shore broke; I want
You to stand *here* —
Or, if you're bored with me,
We can walk up to the Whalers' Cove
Where a few old shacks are left
By a single room-sized caldron
Blackened by its years
Of fires melting acres of fat,
A pot too huge for even the scavengers
To think of carting it away. A local
Fisherman told me it was here
The Russian and his wife
Traded those first hard vows
Made to last longer than a double

Lifetime. Some
Should know better than to promise
Time, or their bodies, even if
Trust lives first in the body
Before rising like an ether
Into the mind. Tonight, waking alone,
I'll walk out into the cold mists
Up to the circular groves
High above the cabin, where the wild
Peacocks primp by the meadows or cry
From their invisible balconies
In the trees, their screams
Those of a child. And
From a prospect
Higher still, where the trees
Begin to grow more sparse and the rocks
More bare, I can look down
Onto the whole of the small harbor,
The bridge lights swaying
Once again, the jetty warning lamps
Blinking along the tower of the unlit
Beacon. The dunes rise and fall
Like shadows of waves down to the bay.
If you had been beside me, sleepless
Or chilled by the sudden violence
Of the winds, maybe you'd have walked
Here with me, or come after

To see what kept me standing in the night —
You'd see nothing. Only, what
Dissolves: dark to dawn, shore to wave,
Wings to fog, a branch to light:
The vague design that doesn't come
From me, yet holds me
To it, just as you might, another time.
And just as the Russian paced here
Rehearsing these lines, looking
Down onto the cove and whalers' shacks
Where she waited drawing a black
Comb out of her hair, I'll
Say for both of us the small prayer
Sworn to live beyond the night:
Until the stars run to milk,
Until the earth divides, until these waves
No longer rake the headland sands,
Until the sea is dead . . . .